49:

A Square of Stories

49:

A Square of Stories

[signature]

Bruce Holland Rogers

For Alex, who adds a very bright
spark. May the acceptances and
publications follow now like a
long, long line of ants!

Whidbey Island

Panisphere Books & Audio

12 August 2013

Panisphere Books & Audio
www.panispherebooks.com

1485 E. Briarcliff Lane
Eugene, OR 97404-3268

Book design by Anne-Marie Lizet.
Cover photo by Stephanie Jadzak.

My darling Nanou,
this book is for you.

Table of Contents

SEVEN

BONUS STORIES

Introduction to the Introduction to the Introduction

My friend Martha says that she often likes the introductions to story collections better than the stories themselves. Stories, she says, are supposed to be attached to a storyteller. The introduction is where she hopes to meet that person.

Martha says that Homer's invocation to the goddess, asking for her help in singing the story of the *Illiad*, reminds us that the poet was right there in front of the audience, in the flesh. When Homer finished his story for the night, the listeners could ask him questions, might even get to know him. The same was true of the *Beowulf* poet, who began by reminding his audience, "we have heard" of the prowess of the Danes. You the audience and I the storyteller, we are embarking on this story together, probably by firelight.

I don't know what Martha thinks of New Criticism generally. That's the movement of the early-to-middle twentieth century that emphasized looking at literary works as self-contained and self-referential constructs. But I do know that Martha thinks New Criticism is still having a bad influence on some English professors. "Pay no attention to those biographical notes about Dickens," say these professors. "Consider the text on its own terms." Martha thinks that's bullshit. Stories don't emerge from a vacuum. The reader of *Little Dorrit* wants to know who Charles Dickens was, wants to meet the person who is speaking.

Martha notes that readers who attend public readings by authors often follow the work of that writer with special interest thereafter. Martha even cites one writer whose work she doesn't particularly like whose books she nevertheless feels attached to because she has heard him read. Now he is one of *her* writers.

Martha says that she likes introductions so much that she'd be happy to read a book of stories that was nothing but introductions. "But not one of your books," she says diplomatically. "I'd want to get to your stories." Of course, Martha already knows me. I am one of *her* writers.

x

Introduction to the Introduction

When it comes to the introductions and other front matter in books, readers tend to fall into one of three camps. There are the Skippers, readers who see front matter as an unnecessary delay. I can't say anything bad about a Skipper, especially a Skipper who is skipping my introduction in order to get right to my stories. Life is short!

In the second camp we find the Dilettantes, readers who will give any piece of front matter a few sentences to prove itself. If Dilettantes are entertained, they keep reading. I have nothing against Dilettantes, and indeed I would like to rehabilitate the word *dilettante*, which we have degraded to mean someone who lacks depth. The word is rooted in the idea of taking delight in things, and I think we're puritanical and joy-killing if we demean the pursuit of delight.

The third camp is occupied by Completists, readers who read every word of a book. Some Completists may be motivated by the anxious fear that they will miss something good in the introduction or maybe even on the copyrights page. No doubt a few Completists are rigid people who feel that to read a book without reading all of the front matter is not to have properly read the book at all. But most Completists, I think, are intellectually voracious. Whatever there is to know, they want to be in on it. I don't have anything bad to say about Completists, either. I probably am one. But I do have a joke about them. In the afterlife, there are two doors. One says "Paradise" and the other says "Lecture About Paradise." The Completists are the people standing in line for the lecture.

If, as my friend Martha supposes, many readers of introductions read them principally to meet the author, what has this text told you about me so far? I like sorting things into categories and giving the categories capitalized names. I do this a lot with my writing students. Recently, one of my students lamented that many of the stories she brought to me for critique had the same flaw: the events happened to the characters, rather than the characters causing the events. Her stories contained wonderful images and ideas, but weren't really under control yet.

I told this student that being a short-story writer is like being a Master of Battle Dragons. There are two main approaches to take with dragons. One is to catch wild dragons and tame them. The advantage to working with a wild dragon is that it's full of fight and surprises. The Master's chief challenge lies in getting enough control to bend the dragon to his will.

Other Masters raise their dragons from eggs and thus have the advantage of working with a tame dragon from the first day. The challenge for such a Master lies in coaxing some fighting spirit and surprises out of a tame creature.

Some writers begin with wild material and have to tame it with strategy and structure. Others start with a structure or strategy and fill that abstract container with enchanting particulars. Either approach can produce excellent work. If a story satisfies, the reader can't tell which came first, the story's useful structure or its lively contents.

Now, what else have I revealed about myself? I see a lot of the world, and a lot of art, in terms of dualities. One key duality is the Wild versus the Tame, or Chaos versus Order. I respect both sides. Also, I don't mind building my metaphors from the stuff of fantasy. I'm not ashamed of my association with dragons. Nor do I make a fetish of dragons (or space ships or hardboiled detectives or historical allusions or allusions to the Bible, fond though I am of all of these). In fact, one of the best ways to get under my skin is to dismiss this or that literary tradition as "inferior."

Really? You can dismiss a whole tradition, an entire generation of writers, or a market category in its entirety? All of it?

Once I was hired by the University of Illinois to teach two fiction workshops for a professor who had been granted a last-minute sabbatical. The director of that writing program said to me, "I am hiring you on the strength of your literary credentials, not your science fiction or mystery writing. If you let the students in these classes write science fiction or detective fiction, you will be undermining something that I have spent years trying to establish." I agreed to the man's terms. I needed the work. But I did all that I could to subvert his prejudice while respecting his fear of what he did not know or understand. Accordingly, many students in my classes wrote literary fiction that dealt with the tropes of aliens or detectives, but they did it with rigor. I insisted on good stories. Category fiction wasn't allowed if you couldn't make it as good, as satisfying to the reader, as the literary stories that other students were submitting. My rule was "Write no crap," but I didn't assume, as the director did, that one could know crap by its parentage.

I love Raymond Carver *and* Raymond Chandler. Poe was brilliant, and so were Melville and Emily Dickinson. Talk trash about Robert A. Heinlein at his worst if you want to —he deserves it. But at his best? At his best, he was funny and inventive and insightful. At his best, he deserves your respect. He has mine. I like fiction written in many traditions. Category romance is disdained by most "serious" readers, including many who never tried it. I have read category romance stories that moved me, that made me a little bit happy and a little bit weepy at the same time. I have finished such a story and thought, *That was well done! How did she do that? Could I pull that off?*

One of the reasons that I especially like flash fiction, the very shortest of stories, is that reading them allows me to move from one tradition to another. I don't like standing still. I *can* stand still long enough to read two novels in the same tradition or by the same author, but just barely.

My difficulty in standing still for the same thing twice extends to my writing, which partly explains why I'm not better known as a writer. When I was still sending my stories out regularly to magazines, I was being published in *The North American Review, Woman's World, The Magazine of Fantasy & Science Fiction, Good Housekeeping, Adbusters, The Sun, Quarterly West, New Mexico Humanities Review, Ellery Queen's Mystery Magazine, and Realms of Fantasy.* I was writing for too many different audiences, it seemed, to have a conventional fiction career.

Oh, and I didn't focus on writing novels. I didn't avoid novels entirely. I'd write one every decade or so. It wouldn't be an obvious fit for the marketplace and wouldn't sell, despite my agent's best efforts. Meanwhile, I'd go back to writing exactly the stories that I wanted to write, sometimes figuring out only after I wrote them what the hell they were and which magazine might want them. I was constantly swimming against the current of what mass publishers want: *More of the same, but different.*

It's easy to understand why publishers (and movie producers) would see this as their formula for success. When we shell out for entertainment, we hate to be disappointed. This is why there are publishing categories and film genres. Labels like "romantic comedy" help the audience who loved *When Harry Met Sally* decide to risk *Sleepless in Seattle*. Readers who have had positive experiences with books in the mystery section but not with books shelved as horror tend to repeat their buying in one part of the bookstore, not the other.

As a writer, I have always felt a stronger pull to *different* than *more of the same*. Or, more accurately, my interests have varied from one day to the next. I have written what I felt moved to write, not what anyone else expected me to produce.

For a long time, this diversity has been my weakness, especially when it's time to put together a new collection of stories. How do I make a collection, a unity, out of my chaotic production?

That's what the forthcoming introduction asks. The pages that follow are top-heavy with theory, may mention writers you haven't heard of, and finish with a recap of my publishing history. Rather than focusing on me as a writer or even my individual stories, the introduction constitutes a lecture about story collections in general and mine in particular.

Dear Reader, you don't have to attend the lecture. There are two doors, and one of them leads directly to stories.

Introduction: The Idea of Order in Collected Fiction

How much order does a short story collection need for the reader to feel that the book is, well, collected? In a book made up of smaller pieces, how much unity and coherence does the reader require? By unity, I mean that every piece in the book has some degree of similarity to every other piece, which might mean that all the stories are written in the same genre, or all the stories might have a similar tone, or they might all be about the same character or be set in the same place and time. By coherence, I mean that each piece rests comfortably against the piece before it and the one that follows it.

How organized, how unified, how coherent, does a collection of stories have to be?

I teach fiction writing in a Master-of-Fine-Arts program. Some of my students write story collections as their theses, and for a few of those students, selection and arrangement of their stories into a book comes easily. Maybe they started with a structural idea: a minor character in each story appears as the protagonist of the next story. Then they wrote stories to fill in that structure. This approach is like sketching the design of a mosaic and only then looking for the colored stones to fill it in. Other students write stories that seem to be part of one whole because each story addresses, in a different way, the one idea that the student feels compelled to keep exploring, such as race relations in 1970s America. And then there are those students who find themselves in a quandary. They wrote their stories, story by story, and may never have considered how to gather them up and present them as some sort of whole. It's as if they were looking at a pile of colored stones, thinking, *What picture can I make from these?*

One helpful-seeming thing I can do is to point out what other writers have done. I can deliver a lecture about how collections must fall somewhere on a spectrum of Order to Chaos. At the orderly extreme is the collection of stories so unified that the writer (or publisher) calls it a "novel in stories." The *most* orderly of such collections favors the "novel" so much that although many of the stories might be able to stand alone, some of them, particularly stories near the end, depend so much on what the reader already knows that these final stories are really *chapters*. An example of such a book is Mark Budman's *My Life at First Try*, which I often include on the reading list of my class in short prose forms precisely because it blurs the lines between a collection and a novel.

Another kind of "novel-in-stories" is one where the orderliness of the "novel" is sacrificed for the sake of good stories. The "novel" may even be an afterthought, as in the case of Ray Bradbury's celebrated *The Martian Chronicles*. That book consists mostly of stories that were meant to be read independently, stories that were first published in magazines. Bradbury later arranged the stories on a timeline of "future history," and he wrote short linking vignettes to braid the stories into this chronology. The patchwork shows. The first few stories feature Martians who are so different from story to story that a reader might reasonably wonder if this is really the same Mars. (Of course, a report of three expeditions of Martians who arrived on earth in Teheran, Rio de Janeiro, and Fairbanks might leave a Martian reader wondering if these expeditions had really gone to the same Earth.)

Bradbury's strategy of first publishing stories individually and then working out a way to present them as a novel was used by quite a few writers in succeeding decades, particularly in science fiction where the markets for short fiction were robust and writers often got their start in shorter pieces. Science-fiction editors and critics called books like *The Martian Chronicles* "fix-up novels."

Bradbury used linking vignettes again with his collection *The Illustrated Man,* and that collection is at a further remove from Order, a step closer to Chaos. In *The Illustrated Man,* the stories aren't arranged by chronology or by common setting. Rather, they share some thematic concerns about the collision of technology and human psychology. The linking device is an unnamed narrator who meets a tattooed vagrant. The tattoos are animated, and each one comes to life to illustrate the next story. Although the narrator's interactions with the tattooed man do have their own arc, the stories themselves can't really be conceived as episodes in a single, greater story. The book is a collection of stories that are connected to one another by yet another story. The linking device doesn't try to make the stories cohere as chapters.

As we move away from the extreme Order of a "novel-in-stories," the principles of unity begin to fragment into different types. Consider, for example, a collection such as Barry Yourgrau's *Wearing Dad's Head.* Yourgrau's collection has unity of characters. Most of the stories feature a nuclear family—the narrator and the narrator's parents. The collection is also unified by chronology: the narrator is a small boy in the early stories, and he and his parents age as the collection proceeds. However, the needs of individual stories trump the collective organizing principle. If an early story requires the death of the parents, they die, even though they will be alive again in the next story. Unlike Budman's *My Life at First Try, Wearing Dad's Head* resolves any conflict between an individual story and the overall arc in favor of the story's independence. *Wearing Dad's Head* has about as much Order as *The Illustrated Man*, but according to an entirely different strategy. Neither book is a fix-up novel, but each is more than "just" stories.

As we move closer to Chaos, Order becomes an organizational principal that we can assess almost by weight. That is, there are different dimensions of unity, and a collection may be heavy with some and light in others. How much is there of each unity? How much unity in total?

I already mentioned that stories could be of the same genre, feature recurring characters, be set in the same locale, or be told in a similar tone. They might also address a common theme, employ a limited set of techniques (every story written mostly in dialog, for instance), or be of similar length. A collection might have unity of several types, as in a collection of novella-length funny fairy tales about dysfunctional families. The same collection feels less orderly if it consists of funny fairy tales *of various lengths* about dysfunctional families. Make half of the stories about politics, rather than family, and you have subtracted several ounces of Order. We could subtract instances of unity until we had a collection utterly chaotic in all of the dimensions we can think of, a collection that brings together stories in which no two narratives share any characteristics beyond having been penned by the same writer.

And would that collection, that assembly of Chaos, be a bad collection?

To answer that question, I need to invoke some of the general principles that I share with my students regarding what readers want.

General principles:
- If readers enjoy the first story, then they hope that the next story will be like that one, so follow like with like.
- But don't put two similar stories together because readers crave variety.
- Also, it's a good idea to follow a poignant story with a funny one. The reader will appreciate the contrast, and the poignant story will seem all the more profound...
- ...unless the reader finds the contrast irritating and thinks you have trivialized something beautiful and deep by putting something comical and superficial after it.
- It works much better to put the funny story first, the poignant one following...
- ...unless the reader finds this upsetting because you essentially dug an emotional trap for the reader, luring him with honey and flowers into the dungeon.
- A collection of only funny stories is an excellent idea, unless it is tiresome.
- Try to think of your collection as a musical concert. Alternate up-tempo with slower pieces.

- Open and close the collection with your two best stories; this strategy works without fail if you are sure which are your two best stories, as determined by the taste of every reader who will ever read your collection.

- Don't mix realistic stories with fanciful ones because the reader won't know how to take you, although if you do mix realistic stories with fanciful ones, some readers will find that mixture delicious and will recommend you to their friends for that very thing, and their friends will be confused by your mix of realism and fantasy and will condemn you for it, and this may even spell the end of that particular friendship.

Again, is it better for a collection to emphasize Order, or Chaos? Consistency, or Surprise? Do stories cohere by being similar, or does contrast actually help to link two stories? Do readers want consistency of tone and technique, or is variety better?

To paraphrase W. Somerset Maugham's maxim about writing a novel, there are three rules to organizing a collection of stories. Unfortunately, no one knows what they are.

I'm not even sure how to assess my own past efforts. *Wind Over Heaven* was edited by Alan Rodgers, who believed that I was essentially a horror writer, so the collection was organized around the question, *Is this horror?* If not, is it at least dark in places? The challenge was to find enough dark stories to fit the editor's label. *Thirteen Ways to Water* was similarly organized by market category, fantasy this time, but some readers have told me that while they liked the individual stories, they regretted reading the book all in one sitting because it was so varied in tone. That is, how readers felt about it depended partly on whether they rested between stories. The third book, *Flaming Arrows,* was illustrated by Alan M. Clark and Jill Bauman, and the illustrations may have helped to unify it. It's out of print now, and I plan on bringing it out myself in a new edition, one without pictures. I don't know yet if the absence of illustrations is going to help or hurt the unity of the new edition. That is, I'm still a bit unsure of *Flaming Arrows* as a collection. Of my first four collections, only *The Keyhole Opera* completely satisfies me as feeling purposeful and just right.

At least I do have that one *collected* collection. And I think I have another one here. I hope so.

So, is *Forty-nine* a pleasing mix of Order and Chaos? Does it strike the right combination of similarity and surprise? Does it follow "the three rules" of organizing a collection? You tell me.

Epilogue to the Introduction

No, that would be silly.

ONE

Dinosaur

When he was very young, he waved his arms, gnashed the teeth of his massive jaws, and tromped around the house so that the dishes trembled in the china cabinet. "Oh, for goodness sake," his mother said. "You are not a dinosaur! You are a human being!" Since he was not a dinosaur, he thought for a time that he might be a pirate. "Seriously," his father said at some point, "what do you want to be?" A fireman, then. Or a policeman. Or a soldier. Some kind of hero. But in high school they gave him tests and told him he was very good with numbers. Perhaps he would like to be a math teacher? That was respectable. Or a tax accountant? He could make a lot of money doing that. It seemed a good idea to make money, what with falling in love and thinking about raising a family. So he was a tax accountant, even though he sometimes regretted that it made him, well, small. And he felt even smaller when he was no longer a tax accountant, but a retired tax accountant. Still worse, a retired tax accountant who forgot things. He forgot to take the garbage to the curb, forgot to take his pill, forgot to turn his hearing aid back on. Every day it seemed he had forgotten more things, important things, like which of his children lived in San Francisco and which of his children were married or divorced.

Then one day when he was out for a walk by the lake, he

forgot what his mother had told him. He forgot that he was not a dinosaur. He stood blinking his dinosaur eyes in the bright sunlight, feeling the familiar warmth on his dinosaur skin, watching dragonflies flitting among the horsetails at the water's edge.

Memoir

True story. It happened like this. During the winter of
'43, the guards would march us out of the camp every
morning to the fields where we worked clearing stones.[1]
We were cold all the time, and hungry.[2] I had gloves, my
salvation.[3] Piotr had cuts on his hands from the stones and the
tools, and week after week the cuts would not heal.[4] I let him
have one of my gloves while we worked together on digging
out a particularly large stone.[5] We dug all the way around
the stone and still could not get it to budge. Exhausted, we
tried to rest. Even when the guards were looking away, we
dared not sit down, but at least we could hold our hands on
our knees for a moment. In this lull, Piotr said, "The war will
be over soon. Remember yesterday, the two men who were
not up for roll call? At first they were to be shot, but they
were hung instead." He looked me in the eye. "The Germans
are running out of bullets!" I don't know why, but that joke
struck me as the funniest thing I had ever heard. I laughed.[6]
Even when one of the guards turned and looked right at us,
I laughed so hard that I had to kneel.[7] Piotr was laughing,
too, and also dropped to his knees, then to his hands and
knees. The guard ran over, leveled his gun at Piotr's head, and
fired.[8] I stopped laughing. I stood up. I said nothing when
other prisoners were called over to take Piotr's body away,
even though it was my glove that the body wore on one hand.

They dragged him by his feet, and I could not take my gaze away from my precious glove.

---

1 For the sake of narrative impact, I have conflated some facts and adjusted others. I was born in 1958, so the date of these events was 1978, not 1943. Also, it wasn't winter. The events took place in April.

2 The college dormitory food service provided 21 meals each week, but if we slept too late on a weekday we would miss breakfast. I frequently missed breakfast.

3 Isotoner men's spandex gloves, knit lined with leather palm strips. The gloves were a gift from my girlfriend's mother at Christmas.

4 Pete DiNicola, my roommate, occasionally cut his fingers because he used a sharp X-Acto knife for his model-rocket hobby. In the story, injuries to his hands explain the loan of my glove.

5 I did not actually lend Pete my glove. I doubt that I had gloves with me at the time. April is not usually cold in Fort Collins, Colorado.

6 To be more precise, Pete and I had gone to the mall to buy some model rocket engines. It was spring. We had girlfriends. We were going to launch his model rocket Saturday. We were skipping our afternoon classes, and we were giddy with the guilty pleasure of playing hooky. Pete told a joke, but I don't remember what it was. The mood we were in, anything would have been funny.

7 At the bottom of the atrium steps, we collapsed in laughter, but not on our knees. We sat down on the steps. The guard was mall security and unarmed, but he did wear a uniform.

8 The guard's exact words were, "Stand up, boys! Cut it out." When we stood up and looked at each other, not sure what rule or code we had violated, the guard said, "You know very well what I mean. If you can't behave in here, I'm going to have to ask you to leave." It was embarrassing. I did stop laughing.

Mysterious Ways

1. Weighed in the Balance

Meena had children to feed and no man in her household. Charity would shame her, so Ismael always gave her a secret discount, nudging the scale up with his thumb. Once, she caught him.

"Thief!"

Bystanders took notice. "And she is a war widow! For shame!"

"My dear lady, if I am cheating you, may God take my right eye!"

The next year, an infection blinded his left eye.

2. Knock and It Shall Be Opened

John's wife got down on her knees beside his hospital bed and prayed for his healing. Holding his hand, she said the words, but John felt them in his heart. Later, the doctors were at a loss to explain his remission and, still later, his complete recovery. Neither could they explain the sudden appearance of his wife's lymphoma, its aggressive spread, its uncanny resistance to all kinds of treatment.

3. Signs and Wonders

An image of the Bodhisattva Maitreya appeared in a tortilla served to Amado Cruz with his breakfast of fruit and beans. The image was absolutely clear to him, though he didn't know who the Bodhisattva was. Just as clear was the visage of the Blessed Virgin on Chemsarpo Kinley's steamy bathroom mirror, which the Bhutanese woman wiped dry just as Amado Cruz, far away, began to eat his miracle.

A Patron of the Arts

It was my custom, after work, to go to a particular café on Rue Queen. There, I always had a café au lait and a tarte aux pommes while I read *Le Devoir*, beginning with the opinion page. The waiter knew what to bring me the moment I sat down. I always left exactly the same tip.

One spring day—the first almost-warm day after a difficult winter—I felt one of those dissatisfactions that can arrive suddenly, like unpleasant weather. I had put on weight during the winter. I was still a bachelor, with no prospects in sight. I was a year older than I had been the previous spring.

What I needed was a change. As I followed my usual path from the office, I resolved to have my café au lait at a different café.

I walked along Rue Saint-Paul, looking for a suitable place. I saw several that were unsuitable—too much for tourists, too brightly lit, too dim. This one was too close to the traffic, and that one was too much in the wind. I continued. One café had an awning that was badly soiled—little details can tell you a lot about a place. If they don't clean their awning, what can the kitchen be like? I grew tired. I began to regret my adventure. But then at last, I found a place that would almost do. If I altered my standards just a bit to allow for the artificial flower on each table, this establishment would suit me.

As I have said, the day was almost warm, warm enough that there were tables and chairs outside. But there was still wind, enough to have driven all the patrons indoors. I went inside only to make sure that I had the waiter's attention, then I sat at the table that was least exposed to wind but still in the sun. I opened *Le Devoir* to the opinion page, and I was halfway through the section when the waiter brought me my café au lait and tarte aux pommes, and I asked for the bill at once. It came to a little more than at my customary café, enough that I did not think I would come here again. I would leave a nice tip, though. It was an opportunity to use up all the change in my pocket.

A man's voice nearby loudly declared, "Mesdames et Messieurs, thank you! Thank you!"

I looked up from my paper. Beyond the farthest table stood a man dressed in an ill-fitting black suit and a red cap. He was looking at me, but then his gaze roamed from table to table, as if there were a great multitude of customers and he were looking into the eyes of each person. "I thank you," he said again. "Please..." He gestured as if asking for applause to cease. "I am, as many of you know, Donat Bobet. Today's recital will be brief..." He held up his hands. "Please, I am sorry, it must be brief today. Two poems only, today. The first is a poem by Alain Bosquet. It is called, 'No Need.'"

The waiter stuck his head out of the door to ask me, "Is he bothering you?"

Had I been planning on becoming a regular at the café, I might have answered in the affirmative. However, as the purpose of coming here was to have a one-time adventure, I said, "Not at all." I folded my newspaper.

"Don't give him any money," said the waiter. And to Monsieur Bobet he said, "If you come among the tables and chairs, it's trespassing!"

"Please," said Bobet. "Please hold your applause until the end."

The waiter went back inside. The poem was a short one about how the designs of animals were sufficient to their needs. An elephant's trunk meant that it needn't stoop, a giraffe's height meant it needn't fly, a chameleon's skin meant it needn't run away, and a turtle's shell meant that it need not find a home. Thus, a poet's poems meant that a poet did not need to understand. Or perhaps it was that a poet didn't need to be understood. As he recited the final line, Donat Bobet made a grand flourish with his hand. He swept the cap from his head and bowed. He said, "Thank you! Thank you everyone! You are too kind."

"I'm not sure I understand it."

"A question?" Bobet cupped a hand to his ear, as if he had just barely heard my voice among the throng of loud admirers.

Absurdly, I raised my voice. "I don't understand it!"

"Ah, well," said Bobet, "understanding isn't everything, is it?" He put his cap back on his head. "Here, for example, is one that you are quite sure not to understand. It is called, 'Afloat on the Saint-Laurent.'" He proceeded then to recite a long poem about the great monuments of Europe floating up the fleuve, toward Lake Ontario. The Brandenburg Gate, the Arc de Triomphe, the Nelson obelisk, among others, all floated in from the sea, against the current. Among them were busts and statues from Athens, from Prague, from

Oslo. When they got to the lake, there they stayed, bobbing on the waves and interfering forever with shipping. At the end, Donat Bobet repeated his grand flourish. He bared his head and bowed. He said, "Thank you! Thank you all so very much. Modesty prevents me from telling you the author of that particular poem. Thank you."

I clapped politely. I picked up my paper and stood.

"As you leave, Mesdames et Messieurs, I would be most grateful for your patronage. Anything at all will help. I mean that quite earnestly. A penny is nothing to you, but to a poet a penny is a portrait of the queen!"

I remembered the waiter's warning not to give the poet anything, but it would be less awkward to settle a few coins on him than to walk by without doing so.

I considered the change I had left on the table for the waiter. There were some pennies there, and quarters, and a dollar coin. But a penny donation was insulting, no matter what Bobet had just said. In any case, it didn't seem right to take from the waiter who had been protective of my solitude, even if I had declined his protection. I opened my wallet and produced a five.

When I handed the bill to Donat Bobet, he looked me in the eyes and said, "Thank you." As I started to walk away, he produced a pen and began to make marks on the bill. He was defacing the portrait of Laurier. He was making the old prime minister smile.

I had gone but a short distance from the café when I heard a shout. "Monsieur! Monsieur!" It was Bobet, running after me, waving the bill. "Fifty! Did you mean to give me so much?"

"Fifty?" I said. We both knew full well what I had given him. But he showed me the five-dollar note. Not only was Wilfrid Laurier smiling, but Bobet had inked in a 0 after each 5. CINQ had been revised to CINQUANTE, and FIVE to FIFTY.

I frowned. "That's no joke. It's one thing to draw on a smile…"

"Fifty!" Bobet said. "Sir, you are a true patron of the arts! I am so grateful! Please, you must dine with me, at my expense. Please! I'll make such a meal. Fifty! I will transport your tastebuds to Indochina! You must say yes! Please say you will do me this honor!"

The waiter had warned me not to give this fellow money, and perhaps Bobet always attached himself to donors. Perhaps he was operating some sort of confidence game. But, of course, I had no confidence in him, so how could he take advantage of me? I could walk away if things took a turn I didn't like. I had no better plans. Day after day, I worked with reasonable, sober people. Hadn't I resolved to have an adventure today? "All right. I consent. But you mustn't try to pass that bill off as the real thing. Not while I'm along."

"My apartment is in this direction," he said, turning me around. "We must stop for a few things along the way. Oh, what a feast we will have!"

We went into a little grocery store. I thought, Ah, here's his game. He'll try to get me to pay for a week's provisions! But Bobet's shopping consisted of a pound of ground chicken and a lime. His five dollars would cover that. As we stood in line, Bobet considered a bouquet of flowers for $6.99. He inspected three different bouquets, then put each one of them back. The cashier rang up the ground chicken, the lime... At the last moment, Bobet reached for one of the bouquets. "After your generosity," he said, "I can afford it!"

He gave the cashier his five dollars and a smile. She hardly looked at the bill, but stood waiting for the rest.

"Well?" said Bobet.

"You're still short," said the cashier.

"My word!" said Bobet. "By how much!"

The cashier looked at the total. "Six dollars and seventeen cents."

Bobet shook his head. "The price of luxurious living!" He looked at me. "I am not accustomed to spending so freely. I'm afraid your donation went to my head. I suppose we can do without the flowers."

Flowers. Was that all he would try to take me for? I was grateful that he hadn't insisted to the cashier that he had given her fifty dollars. I opened my wallet. I have him ten. He paid, accepted the cashier's change, and then did not pocket the money as I expected. He gave the change to me. "I am so embarrassed," he said. "I am behind the times. I thought fifty would carry us much further. But no matter. We will still have our feast!"

We walked together up Rue Saint-François-Xavier. I didn't see how he could afford to live in this neighborhood. Then we took a side street and came to a building with cracks in the old stone walls. Several of the windows were painted over. Bobet opened the lobby doors with a key, then stood still.

"Oh, what am I thinking?" he said. "We need wine. I'm

sorry. Would you do me the favor of picking some up? There is an SAQ nearby." He told me how to walk to the liquor store.

I went out and bought the wine. I bought a nice Chardonnay since I expected that I might drink it alone. Bobet did have a key to that tumble-down building, but what of it? He might have stolen it. He might have run to the end of his game with me. I wasn't positive that the man actually lived anywhere but on the street.

When I returned, though, I found his name behind the cracked glass of the apartment directory.

"Third floor," he said when I buzzed. "Mine is the apartment with the magnificently ornate carved doors. You'll know them when you see them. The other apartments... Well, my neighbors don't keep their places up as I do."

I found the stairs. The stairwell was lit with a naked bulb. There were certainly no ornately carved doors on the second floor. The doors and hallways were dirty yellow. I wondered if they had been painted within the last century.

I did not see any unusual doors on the third floor, either. Just the same yellow paint, the same dented doorknobs. Finally, at the end of the hallway, a door that was just like all the others had something written on it, like graffiti. It said, "Magnificent ornately carved doors of an oriental motif."

It made me smile. I knocked.

Bobet came to the door wearing an apron. "Dinner is well underway!" he said. "Shall we open the wine to let it breathe?"

"It's a Chardonnay," I said. "We can drink it at once."

"But come in, come in!" He waved me inside and took the wine from me. "Please, have a look around."

Just inside the door, the walls of the brief hallway were marked with big squares and rectangles, each with more graffiti in the same hand that had labeled the front door. Inside one rectangle was written, "The Bog in the Forest by Fedor Vassiliev." Next to that was one that said, "The Pond at Montgeron, Claude Monet." The apartment was nothing more than a hallway leading to a single room with a table and chairs in one corner, a stove in another, and a bed in the third. Here the imaginary paintings were "By Alexander Mordvinov, View of the Grand Canal in Venice, Midday," "Garden at Giverny, Claude Monet."

"As you can see," Bobet said as he worked at the stove, spoon in hand, "I have a passion for the Russians."

"And Monet," I observed.

"Monet, of course! Monet is a god! I would love to have one of his haystacks..."

"You still have some wall space," I said.

"But not the money," Bobet said. "Not yet." He laughed. "Although now that I have met a wealthy patron..."

On the floor, inside another rectangle, were the words, "Persian carpet of black, gold, red, and white, in a fine geometric pattern." The simple wooden chair against one wall said, "Overstuffed armchair. Red."

I sat in the red chair. I smiled. In truth, I felt a bit as if I truly were a wealthy patron of the arts. I rubbed my belly. There was a much slimmer me inside of there, underneath the winter fat. Actually, it was several winters of fat. Bobet was furiously stirring three pans on the stove. I said, "It smells good." And it did. Whatever he was doing with the ground chicken smelled rich and exotic.

The flower bouquet sat in the middle of the table in a mason jar labeled "cut crystal." The biggest window in the room looked onto the alleyway, but written on the pane were the words, "view of the Saint-Laurent." Bobet opened the wine and poured it into two glasses. "Come, come!" he said.

I rose from the overstuffed armchair. Bobet served our dinners on unmatched but elegant china plates. Each plate held a mound of rice which, judging from the bits of peas and carrots, had been an element of an earlier meal. I overlooked that. The ground chicken had been divided into thirds, each cooked in its own spices. A flower garnished each plate.

We ate. I detected lemon grass and red pepper in one portion, lime and coriander in another. In the third, I tasted a bit of garlic, and perhaps a hint of ginger. All three were marvelous.

I relaxed. I looked about the room. "Is that incense burner really an antique?" It was made of folded aluminum foil. Written on one relatively unwrinkled surface were the words, "Tang dynasty bronze."

"Oh, yes," said the poet. "I inherited it. My family had money at one time." He lifted his wineglass. "To art and artists," he said.

"But I am no artist."

"My friend, you most certainly are," said Donat Bobet. "What is more, you are a rich patron, a man admired for his taste and generosity. I salute you!"

I took up my wine glass. With my free hand, I imitated the flourish Bobet had made with his hand when he finished reading a poem. I said, "I thank you!"

We drank. In time, we finished the bottle. At some point, I asked, "So how much do you need, to keep all of this up?"

"Oh," he said, "an occasional gift of fifty, just as you gave me today..."

That is how I became one of the principal patrons of the Montreal poet, Donat Bobet, and how it became my custom to dine with him, every now and then.

Daddy

Peg said to me, "You're sure you want to come? They don't always know until the blood tests come back." But I wanted to take the day off. This was an occasion. Besides, it was a beautiful day. There wasn't a cloud in the sky. We took a streetcar, then walked two blocks. In the trees over Chester Avenue, squirrels frolicked and robins chirped. I saw people walking jolly dogs. Sunlight glinted on the windshields of parked cars. I held Peg's hand.

The nurse called Peg's name and took her to see the doctor. When Peg reappeared, she had a smile for me. "They'll call when they get the lab report. But the doctor says she can already tell. I am. You're going to be a daddy."

I smiled. I kissed her. As we walked hand in hand to the streetcar stop, I noticed again that there wasn't a cloud in the sky, and I remembered that sunlight can give you cancer. I wished for an umbrella. The trees over Chester Avenue were full of squirrels and robins. The fleas on squirrels can transmit plague. Birds made me think of West Nile virus. And all these dogs... Any one of them can bite, can carry rabies. As we crossed the street, I glared at the drivers. Sharp chrome. Glass. Peg said, "You're hurting my hand." I said I was sorry, and I lessened my grip. But not much.

China Moss

Driving north on U.S. 36, Larry crested the rise and Boulder Valley unfolded before him: the towers and red tile roofs of the university, a leafy canopy of urban trees, the reddish sandstone flatirons and dark pine foothills with mountains behind, all under the intense blue of the Colorado sky. He sighed.

From the passenger seat, his daughter said, "What?" She was checking her hair for split ends.

"Nothing," he said.

Austin kept fiddling with her hair.

Into the silence, he added, "It's been a long time since I've seen that view," he said. "It's like Oz." Boulder was still beautiful. It had changed, though. "But Boulder isn't what it was when your mother and I went to school here."

"Mom says that, too," Austin said. She looked at the view. For her, there was only the city of now, Boulder without layers underneath of a city that once had been. She said, "Fewer hippies, huh?"

"Or artists or musicians. That's part of it, I guess."

"So what do you miss the most?"

The question surprised Larry. In the last four years, Austin had made it clear she had no interest in his opinions. "You really want to know?"

She make a clicking sound with her tongue. "No, I just asked because I like to hear myself talk." Larry couldn't look away from the road, but he was sure she was rolling her eyes.

"I miss lots of things." He thought about eating at the communal table at The Harvest, recovering from a hangover with greasy eggs at The Aristocrat, or having a beer with the regular guys at Tom's. He missed the feel of the place, a vibe that had faded with time.

Austin said, "Okay. Forget I asked."

"China moss," he said. "I miss China moss."

"Is that a restaurant?"

"It's a dessert. There used to be a restaurant in a converted house, the Indo-Ceylon. It's where I used to like to take my dates. Really good food. At the time, it was exotic for Boulder."

"Did you take Mom?"

"More than once. China moss was a gelatin dessert."

"You miss Jell-o?" Austin made the sound—almost a snort—that she reserved for parental absurdities.

"No. Not Jell-o. It was a cube in two layers with different textures. One layer was fruity, like mango or guava or something, with a very distinctive texture. Later I figured out it must be made with isinglass."

"What's isinglass?"

They had followed the highway down into the bowl of the valley, and Larry took the exit for Austin's dormitory, her new home until Christmas break. "Its texture is both smooth and grainy."

"It will take me about two seconds to find out what isinglass is," Austin said. "I'll Google it."

"The other layer was some other kind of gelatin, more like Jell-o, but flavored with coconut milk. The contrast of flavors and textures... Heaven. That's what I miss the most. I miss being able to go into the Indo-Ceylon for dinner and China moss."

"The restaurant closed?"

"Before you were born."

"I bet you could find a recipe on the web."

"It wouldn't be the same," he told her. What he missed was impossible to recover. Austin wouldn't understand that yet.

The first time Austin called him from school, in September, she needed more money for books than she had budgeted for. The second time, it was just because she wanted to talk, and she let slip that she had tried her mother first, but Marie wasn't home. In October, the third call began with the words, "I found out what isinglass is, and I think it's disgusting."

At first, he couldn't imagine why she was calling him about isinglass.

"But guess what? I found a place with China moss on the menu. Want to come to dinner?" When he hesitated, she added, "My treat." He thought of making a joke about being treated with his own money, but he held his tongue. She was on a tight budget. Her invitation was generous.

"Okay," he said. "But it won't be the same. It just won't."

Bruce Holland Rogers

"We'll see," she said as if she were holding a secret. "We'll see."

The story of the restaurant was printed right on the menu. The owner was a Peace Corps volunteer who had returned to the U.S. with a Sri Lankan wife. For the last twenty years, he had been a school teacher. Retired from that job, he was returning to the restaurant business with the same menu that had once been so popular.

As Larry considered the list of curries, Austin said, "Look familiar?"

Pork curry. Chicken curry. Vegetable curry. Crab curry. Fish curry with three stars and a warning, VERY HOT SPICE! "It looks just the same."

"And you'll notice, under the desserts..."

There it was. China moss.

They ordered an assortment of curries, and as they ate, Larry considered their surroundings. It was a Friday night, and the restaurant wasn't busy. The old location, in a converted house, had a charm that an ordinary restaurant couldn't match. At the old place, too, the tables were few, so the number of reservations available on any night was very limited. Part of what made it special was scarcity. In those days, too, the night air felt different. October air used to be full of possibility.

"I've been here twice before with friends," Austin said. "We love it! Is it like you remember?"

"It tastes good," Larry said.

He asked Austin about school, and she rattled on about

her classes and her teachers. By the time she slowed down, they had finished the curries. Austin hadn't spoken as many words about school during three years of high school, at least not to Larry. He decided not to make this observation aloud. Instead, he said, "So you like school so far."

"Eh, it's okay," she said, as if remembering to be a teen.

The waiter came to ask about dessert, and Austin called for two China moss. "That is what you want," she said after the waiter had gone, "right?"

"Did you have it when you came before?" he said.

"No. I'm saving it to try with you. I hope you're wrong about isinglass." She made a face. "Fish bladders?"

"Swim bladders. And Jell-o is made from hooves. You lived on that stuff when you were a kid."

The desserts arrived. They looked just as Larry remembered, white underneath, pink translucence above. He picked up his spoon and hesitated. He looked at Austin.

"You first," she said.

He gave her a little smile. "I'm not sure I want to," he said.

"Why not? You said this was what you missed the most from Boulder!"

"I know. The thing is..." He looked at her. She didn't look any different from how she had looked when he drove her to the dormitory in September, or when she had come to see him on alternate weekends over the last seven years. "What if I taste it, and it's not as good as I remember?"

"You'll get over it."

He smiled at that. That had been his line to his daughter more than once. However, getting over things was part of the problem. He had lost jobs, failed at marriage, failed at love again after that. Those were things you got over. Nonetheless, disappointments still cost him something, even the small ones.

"We'll both take a bite, on three," he said. With his spoon he sliced off a corner of China moss.

Austin did the same.

He counted to three, closed his eyes, and lifted the spoon to his mouth. The confection was sweet, a little tart, fatty, grainy, rubbery, smooth. Exotic, familiar, and just right. With his eyes closed, he could have been twenty-one again and sitting across from the young version of Marie, or maybe Debbie Moran or Cheryl Lechleitner. He was young and good-looking and full of promise.

He opened his eyes to find that Austin still hadn't taken her bite. She said, "Well?"

"It's exactly as I remember," he said. Suddenly sorrow tugged him down like an anchor chain around his ankles. Why such sadness? It was as if the recovery of this particular pleasure, this taste and texture, was another kind of loss, one that he hadn't known was possible. Austin's face blurred, as did everything else in the room. Larry wiped his eyes. "It's great."

"Really? Looks to me like it's so bad it brings tears to your eyes!"

He laughed. The sound came out ragged. "I'm a lucky guy. Here I am, having dinner with a beautiful woman. And she's young enough to be my daughter!"

Austin rolled her eyes. She would lose that gesture

eventually. The world would keep changing, his daughter along with everything else.

You fall in love, he thought. What you love falls away. Everything and everyone is falling away, or is going to fall, and it breaks your heart. Again. And again and again.

Larry wiped his eyes one last time. He took a breath. He felt light. He felt sad and happy and strong.

"Daddy," Austin said. She hadn't called him Daddy in years. "Are you okay?"

"I am," he said. He blew his nose. "I'm okay, and then some."

She lifted her spoonful of China moss. "It's that good, is it?"

He said, "It's that good. All of it. And sometimes, I even notice."

Donat Bobet in Africa

When I had known the poet Donat Bobet for a few months, he said to me at dinner one night, "I am going to Africa. Perhaps you would like to come?"

"To Africa?" I said. "How ever will you afford it?" This was, of course, a foolish question. Bobet had his patrons, after all, his means to making things happen.

"We will depart from my apartment on Thursday night," he said, "at half past seven." It was Tuesday.

"Very well," I said. I had nothing else to do. I might as well go to Africa, especially as I assumed that I could get back to Montreal in time for work on Friday morning. "What shall I pack?"

"That is up to you," said Donat Bobet. "A toothbrush. A clean shirt. A gun if you wish to hunt."

"It's to be a hunting safari, then?"

"That's customary," said the poet. "We'll see how people feel about it."

"People?"

"Many of my patrons are coming," he said. "You'll get to meet the rest of Montreal society, though I imagine you know them already."

In fact, I was a mid-level manager. I didn't know Montreal

society. But then, neither did Bobet. All of his patrons were, I felt sure, people like me, people who gave him a few dollars now and then.

On the appointed night, I arrived a little late. Inside a rucksack I carried a clean shirt and a toothbrush. No gun. When I knocked on Bobet's door a girl of about nineteen answered.

"Welcome to Africa," she said. Pinned onto her dress was a sheet of paper with the word, "elephant."

Littering the apartment's brief hallway was an assortment of rucksacks and small suitcases.

"You can leave your bag," the girl said. "You won't need it on the savannah." I set my bag among the others.

There were at least a dozen loudly conversing guests in the room that served as Bobet's living room, bedroom, and kitchen. People stood or sat on cushions—Bobet had only four chairs—and wore sheets of paper labeled, "cape buffalo," or "lion," or "gazelle." I saw a spotted hyena apparently flirting with a young crocodile. Every animal held a wine glass or an hors d'œuvre. Some of them held books or sheaves of paper as well.

Only Bobet wore no label. When he saw me come in, he cried out, "Attention! Your attention everyone!" The conversations quieted some. Bobet lifted a pair of binoculars and inspected me through them. "A brown hyena!" he called out. "Shy, solitary, and increasingly rare!"

"Brown hyena!" called out the guests, raising their glasses. "To the brown hyena!"

Conversations resumed as the elephant pinned a "brown hyena" label onto my shirt.

"Your attention again, please! Attention!" said Bobet. "And now that all the animals are assembled, it is time for the hunt!" He opened a cardboard box and removed from it...a revolver.

At that, the conversations quieted again, considerably. As Bobet overturned the box on his table and a handful of bullets spilled out, the remaining conversations halted altogether.

One of the bullets rolled onto the floor.

"My God," the gazelle said.

"Donat!" said a white rhino. "What do you have in mind?"

"Tradition! The big game hunt is a customary part of African adventure," said Bobet. He swung out the cylinder and slid the first bullet into place. I did not doubt that this was a real gun.

Those were real bullets. I began to consider what I knew of Donat Bobet. Did I know him well enough to be confident that he was merely a bit eccentric, merely a man of imagination? The second bullet slid into place. The third. The fourth. I looked around the room. Other guests were doubtless having the same thoughts as I was. No one moved.

"Elephant," said Bobet, "will you be a dear and fetch me the round that rolled under that chair? There where the lion is sitting?"

Without hesitation, the girl brought the bullet to Bobet. He loaded the fifth chamber, then the last one. He snapped the cylinder into place. "What is it, this pleasure of killing for sport, for entertainment?" He aimed the gun at elephant, who had just brought him a bullet, then at crocodile, then at me. I took a step back, but the gun lingered. The hole in the end looked immense.

Bobet continued around the room, aiming at one guest after another.

"Donat!" someone whispered. "Stop this!"

"Mesdames et Messieurs, we are conducting an experiment into the nature of blood sport, and I must tell you, when I look down the sights of a loaded gun at the innocent eyes of a zebra—" He aimed at the zebra, who stared back at him, frozen. "—I find myself disgusted." He lowered the gun, cracked open the cylinder, and spilled the bullets into the box. "With a little imagination, we recognize that killing for pleasure is a despicable practice, do we not?"

I had stopped breathing. I started again.

"Instead of shooting the animals," said Bobet, "I would like to invite them to read us some poetry. Who would like to go first?"

"Donat," said a woman, "you are fucking insane." She tore off her animal label and made for the door. She turned, expecting others to follow her. But no one did. "And all the rest of you are fucking crazy, too!"

When she had gone, the white rhino volunteered to read a poem. I have no talent for poetry appreciation. I can't tell good poetry from bad. But during the rhino's reading, during all the poems that were read aloud that night, my attention did not stray as it normally might have done. I was there. I was present. There under the African sun, I heard every line.

TWO

Acknowledgments

A book like this one is never the work of only the author, and I want to especially acknowledge the assistance of three people.

Dr. Erika Margarite Schnelvogel, Director of Semiotics and Linguistic Studies at McKenzie University, who retrieved a dictionary from a shelf that was too high for me to reach.

Dr. Lance Trout, formerly Assistant Professor at the Interdisciplinary Research Institute of McKenzie University, whose close association with a series of undergraduate women, faculty wives, and the underage daughter of the Dean of Faculty opened up a tenure-track research position at McKenzie University.

Mr. Ernest "Burnsie" Woodside, proprietor of Burnsie's Bait and Tackle, who told a joke to Ed Macky, who told it to Vernon Pinnock, who told it to two irritable lumberjacks one night at Tooby's Tavern. The resulting fight spilled out of the bar and continued on Highway 99 as an exchange of gunfire. During my commute to McKenzie University the next morning, a State Patrol cruiser was parked, lights flashing, near the site of the crash, causing me to brake before a series of curves. I had been distracted, composing a chapter in my head, and had I not braked the consequences might have been fatal to this book.

Bruce Holland Rogers

In the cascade of causality, it is difficult to name with certainty anyone who did not in some way contribute to or interfere with my efforts. For whatever is good and correct in my text, I am grateful to those named above and to the countless others whom I am unable to cite individually, let alone enumerate. As for any inaccuracies or errors, who is to say, dear reader, that these are not your own fault?

Donat Bobet Administers a Test

It was May. Donat Bobet and I strolled across the Parc Jeanne-Mance among the university students with book bags on their shoulders, the young mothers pushing strollers, the office workers like me enjoying a midday respite. I saw a man selling ice cream out of a little cart. "Would you care for an ice cream, Donat?"

"I adore ice cream!" he said. "Lamentably, I find that I cannot eat it on an empty stomach." He rubbed his belly.

Though I had eaten lunch before joining him, I led him to a café where he ordered a sandwich, a salad, and a beer. I paid the bill even before he was obliged to examine his wallet and find it, sadly, empty. We returned to the park. I bought an ice cream for each of us.

"Thank you," said the poet.

"Well," I told him, "I must maintain my reputation as a faithful patron of the arts."

"Patron of the arts," he repeated, making it sound almost like a question. "Patron of the arts." He turned suddenly on the path. "And how is it," he said in an accusatory tone, "that I have never seen you attempt poetry yourself?"

I thought his manner was rather aggressive, especially toward a friend who had just bought him lunch, a friend who had bought him the ice cream that he now shook in my face.

He said, in the manner of an inquisitor, "Have you written poems, yet not shown them to me?"

"My friend," I said. I gestured helplessly with my own ice cream. "I have shown you no poems because there are none to show. I am no poet, Donat. I haven't the aptitude."

He scowled and turned away. I hurried along behind. The poet now ate his ice cream in great bites, as if the confection were the object of his disdain. When he had finished, he still marched through the park without looking back at me. Finally, he turned from the path and started across the grass.

"Where are we going?"

Donat stopped in the middle of a grassy expanse. He lay on his back, stretching his hands out to either side. "Come," he said. "Lie down."

I finished my ice cream, then wiped my fingers with my handkerchief. "Is the ground quite dry?" I said. "I have to return to work soon."

"Patron of the arts," Donat said. "Patron of the arts." Then he said, "Monsieur, it is one thing to buy a poet an ice cream. But you will not risk dampness to your business clothes for the sake of art?"

I felt the grass with my hands. I do not know what I would have done if I had concluded that it was too damp. However, the lawn posed no danger to my clothes. I lay down on my back.

"Arms out," Donat said. "Hold onto the grass."

I did as he commanded.

"When I was a boy," Donat said, "I was afraid of falling

into the sky. And you? Were you ever afraid of falling into the sky?"

I made no reply. The idea was absurd. No one falls into the sky, and surely even as a child I had sense enough not to fear such a thing.

"Look up," said Donat.

Lying on my back, I really had nowhere to look but up. Little fat clouds wandered the springtime sky.

"What is gravity, the force that holds you to the earth? A mystery, no? Can you rely on it, this mysterious force?"

"I do rely on it, Donat."

"Close your eyes, Monsieur. Close your eyes."

I closed them.

"Consider what it would be like to fall into the sky. All that blue space. The distances between the clouds. A man falling into the sky might fall forever!"

I felt ridiculous. I began to wonder who might be watching us.

"When I was a child," said Donat Bobet, "I would lie in the grass and imagine myself falling up, up, up into the blue. Into the blue depths of the sky. Into the blue."

"Donat..." I said.

"Hush," said the poet. He said nothing for the space of a few heartbeats. "Get ready," he whispered. "Open your eyes!"

When I opened my eyes, I saw above me the blue sky, the little clouds. I saw Donat Bobet, on his knees, watching me.

"The sky," said Donat. "Falling into the sky!"

I examined the airy deep. I considered the clouds. I considered, not very seriously, the absurd idea of falling up.

41

Suddenly, my stomach turned, as it does when an elevator descends. I felt the earth lose its grip. I clutched the grass in my fists. Clenched my jaw.

I was dizzy. I tore the grass free in my fists. My head spun.

I turned onto my side to regain my equilibrium. No good. My stomach still twisted.

I sat up.

The world righted itself.

Donat Bobet was laughing. He pulled me to my feet and embraced me. He shook with laughter. "Your face!" he said. "Oh, the terror in your eyes! The terror!"

He kissed me on each cheek. He embraced me again.

I still felt a little dizzy.

The poet took a step back. He made his face stern. "Never!" he said, pointing like an offended schoolmaster at my chest, "Never again say that you have no aptitude for poetry!"

Three Soldiers

1. The Hardest Question

My marines bring me questions. "When do we get to shower?" "Sergeant, how do you say 'Good afternoon' again?" "Sarge, where can I get more gun oil?"

I have answers. "Tomorrow, maybe." "*Maysuh alheer.*" "Use mine."

Answering their questions is my job. But when Anaya was shot and bleeding out, he grabbed my arm and said, "Sergeant? Sergeant?" I understood the question, but damn. I didn't have an answer.

2. Foreign War

No U.S. soldier who could see that kid would have shot him. But that's long-range ordnance for you. Calder stood next to me in the street, looking at the pieces. "We've come so far from home," he said, "that we'll never get back."

"You dumbass," I said. But a year later, I stood on the tarmac hugging my child, thinking of that kid in pieces, and I wasn't home.

3. Decisions, Decisions

In morning twilight far away, my men are making up their minds:

What's that guy carrying?

Friend or foe?

I should be there, helping them decide. My wife and my parents do their best to make Christmas dinner conversation around my silence. An hour ago, I was yelling at Angie for turning on the damn news. My father, carving, won't meet my eyes. He says, "White meat, or dark?"

Extended Family

The man in the embassy sits on the other side of a counter and we speak through a window with holes in it, as if this were a bank. He looks at the letter I have given him with my papers. I tell him again who the woman in his country is to me. We are sisters.

He says, "Sisters?" He speaks with an accent.

"Sisters." During the war, I explain, my father died, and a man who was kind to my mother and brought her things that we needed, he became my new father. In a year, my brother was born. I helped. I washed out my brother's diapers and hung them on the wall of what used to be our neighbor's house. I watched him and tried to make him sleep when my mother had to go out. Every day she and my new father looked for things that we needed. They traded. They bargained. My new father was especially good at this. But one day, my mother went out to see if she could find milk, and she didn't come home. People disappeared all the time.

After a while, I had a new mother. She was young and pretty. My father brought her to live with us. When the invasion was happening, people who were not soldiers came in the night with guns and took my father away. Later, we found him hanging from a lamp post. Life was even harder after that, when it was just the three of us, my baby brother, my new mother, and me. It was hard to find enough to eat, and especially hard to find milk for the baby. He was sick all the time.

During the occupation, my new mother made friends with one of the soldiers. That saved us. He brought things for us. Milk powder. Cans of food. Sometimes chocolate. Some of the soldiers, they were nice when they were here, but then they left women behind. Not him. Not this man who married my mother and became my new new father.

When my sister was born, my mother was weak at first, and my new father could not be with us all the time. I took care of everyone: my mother, my little brother and my baby sister. I could carry my sister on my hip and lead my brother around by the hand. I did the cooking. I did whatever was needed.

The occupation ended, and my mother and father took my sister to my father's country. My brother and I had to stay behind, in the orphanage, even though we had a family. We never saw our parents again.

My brother died years ago. I looked for my parents, but they are dead, too. I have only my sister, living in my father's country. I want to see her again. I want to have what is left of my family. I need a visa.

The man on the other side of the window listens to all this. He still holds the letter from my sister. He says, with his strong accent, "But you are not related."

I think it is a matter of words. I think, because of his accent, that he has not heard me clearly. But as it turns out, he understands my words. The problem is something else. He does not know what is a family.

The Two Musketeers

One evening I met Donat Bobet in a bar on the Rue Jolicoeur to enjoy a bottle of wine with bread and cheese. I thought I would amuse him with the solecisms of a young American woman who lived in my building. I reminded him of the English word, *jolly*, which someone might mistakenly imagine was related to the French, *jolie*. "For the entire first month after her arrival in Montreal, whenever someone asked her how she was, she said that she was very pretty!"

My companion stared into his wine. The corners of his mouth turned up in only the faintest hint of a smile.

"You see," I said, "she meant to say that she was very happy."

"Do you doubt it?" asked Donat Bobet.

"She seems happy enough. That's not the point."

He looked up from his wine. "Do you doubt that she is very pretty?"

"She's a lovely girl."

"Well, then." He asked if I didn't want some more of the cheese. I declined. This was only an appetizer for me, but I thought that for Donat, wine and cheese were to be the whole of his dinner.

"Here's another example," I said. "A better one. When

Mme Leon across the hall asked this girl what her plans were for the summer, she said that she and her family intended to make a crusade."

"Alas!" said the poet. "As if there were not enough troubles in the world! As if there have not been too many wars already!"

"They aren't making war at all, Donat. She was trying to say that they were going to take a cruise."

"You're sure?"

"Of course I'm sure! Mme Leon told her the right word. At least the girl is able to laugh at herself. I would be mortified if I were trying to speak English and made such an error."

"A crusade. What a disgrace. But you might dress up and carry flags. Colors flying in the wind!" He filled his glass from the bottle and added some more to my glass as well. He was always meticulous about equal shares of wine even though I always paid the whole of the bill.

"Don't you find these errors amusing?"

"Ah, what is an error, after all?"

"Last week, she went on and on about how upset she was that the building manager had not restored the musketeers to her windows. She meant the window screens, of course."

He no more laughed at this example than he had at the others. He narrowed his eyes and said, "Are you quite sure?"

It was perhaps two weeks later when the poet rang and asked me to buzz him in. He appeared in the corridor outside my apartment with some sort of green fabric draped over his arm. He also had two wooden pop guns with corks sticking out of their barrels. "It took some doing," he said, "to find suitable dress." He put down the guns and showed me that

48

the fabric was actually two tabards of the sort that a grocer might wear. There was a big pocket for the grocer's pencil and box cutter. Above the pocket, someone had painted each tabard with a white cross and fleur-de-lis, the insignia of the royal guard. The musketeers.

"Let's put them on," he said. "Which way to the American's apartment?"

The American tenant laughed until there were tears in her eyes. She went across the hall to get Mme Leon. I still have the photograph that Mme Leon took of us guarding her neighbor. Although I couldn't help but smile for the camera, the poet posed with a stern expression. He said, "Is it really so absurd that a young woman living alone in the city might want musketeers for her windows?"

Later, as we walked back to my apartment for a glass of wine, I said, "That was some joke, Donat."

"That was serious business," he said. "Mademoiselle must be commended for her imagination."

"What imagination? She mixed up the word."

"My friend," said Donat Bobet, "the poem does not care whether the poet intended to write it or not."

Away From It All

When Geoff crawled out of bed at three because it was his turn to feed Dylan, or when he took Brynn along for grocery shopping and she screeched at the top of her little lungs so that everyone in the Sainsbury's produce section turned to look, he dreamed of a boarding school for infants and toddlers. Somewhere in Iceland, say. Or Siberia. His team of classmates at the business school seemed not to understand his distraction and didn't tolerate his occasionally late contributions to their projects. Meanwhile, Dylan didn't tolerate his mother's milk or any alternative they tried. He was an ascended master of projectile vomiting. Just when Geoff and Julie started to hope that he was going to keep down this feeding of goat's milk or formula, he would geyser up a creamy jet. Geoff thought more than once, *Dear God, look at what my life has become.*

On the other hand, there was that Sunday morning after a bad night when Geoff woke up to a full bed. Dylan slumbered with his hand closed on his mother's breast and Brynn sprawled on her back, arms wide as if to embrace everything that life would offer. Julie's hair was a tangle of beautiful chaos. Geoff very carefully kissed each sleeping head, crept out of bed, and turned again to admire them. He thought, *I can't believe this is my life.*

That was the march of days and nights. Some good. Some not. He envied the bachelors in his class. He eyed the single women, speculating. He slept on the Tube. Sometimes he missed his stop. At home, he'd open the door to the emotional lottery. What would it be tonight? Everyone in tears? Or the rare report that Dylan had kept something down, and Julie bouncing her good baby on her knee while Brynn entertained her brother with a song?

On the morning of the final project presentation, already late, Geoff rushed his farewells at the breakfast table. He kissed Julie's ear. He kissed Brynn and told her to be good for Mummy. And when he turned toward Dylan, the baby nailed Geoff's shirt, coat and tie from three feet away.

"Sorry, sorry, sorry," he told his team. He stumbled through his part of the market analysis wearing his second-best suit and wondering if he didn't still smell of baby puke. The presentation after theirs was led by a student from Japan, Michiko Higa. Geoff's head grew heavy on his neck. He let his eyes close, and he lay with his head on Michiko's lap while she stroked his ear. Warm cherry blossoms fell on them both while he slept. He woke when his chin hit his chest. Michiko was still at the front of the room talking about modular product customization, and Geoff looked around, wondering if he had snored.

Later, he had a funny idea. At least, he thought so at the time. He printed a photo of Mount Fuji on card stock to make a postcard, and he addressed it to Julie. *Darling,* he wrote, *I have run away and joined the circus. We are touring Japan. The cherry blossoms are lovely. This is the life for me. I'm sure you understand.* He signed it, then went to find Michiko Higa to see if she could arrange for it to come from Japan with the proper stamp and postmark.

The next day, he wasn't so sure of the joke. He tried to remember exactly what he had written. Some days Julie had a sense of humor, and some days she didn't. But Michiko had already sent the card to her family.

Day after day, Geoff came home and found chaos, or chaotic bliss. In two weeks, he thought the card probably should have arrived by now. Julie never mentioned it, not even when Geoff asked if there had been any interesting mail. After a month, Geoff thought with a mixture of relief and disappointment that Michiko's family must have neglected to post the card.

Then, one evening, mixed in with the other mail at his place at the table, Geoff found a picture postcard from Brazil addressed to him in Julie's hand. *Mommy's gone away*, it said. *I never really wanted children. Now I live for samba. I dance all night and sleep through the days. I will love you always, but it's better this way.*

Geoff put the card in his pocket. Later, he put it in the cigar box where he kept assorted treasures. He said nothing about the card. He sent his next one four months later. In that card, he was living as a fisherman in Alaska. The work was hard and dangerous, but none of the crew cried when they had to eat peas. The next card from Julie came from a beach in Australia where no one asked anything of her from first light to last.

Sometimes they went years between cards, but then one of them would remember. When Brynn was in high school, she handed the mail to her father with a postcard on top.

"Mum wasn't really in Thailand, was she?" Geoff was about to say, *It's just a joke,* but he didn't want to. It wasn't only a joke. Fortunately, Brynn didn't insist on an explanation. Her parents were in their forties, and old people did strange, uninteresting things.

After that, as long as the children were still living at home, Geoff and Julie sent their cards to each other's work addresses. Geoff wondered if any rumors circulated about him in Julie's office, or if anyone in the mail room really thought that his wife had left him for a much younger and richer man in Vienna.

At the rehearsal dinner for Dylan's wedding, the father of the bride noted how few of the older couples were still with their first spouses. Geoff and Julie were the exception. "What's the secret?" he asked. Dylan and his sister, now a mother herself, laughed at what they thought was their mother's joke when Julie said, with the barest smile, "Separate vacations."

Consulting Fee

Ed was chopping carrots and summer squash when Susan came home. She put on an apron and checked the open cookbooks to see what they were making. She took the package of chicken thighs from the refrigerator and started to rinse the pieces in the sink.

"Good day at work?" he asked.

"It was all right. How was your day?"

"So far, so good," he said. He had spent the afternoon studying. In two hours, his bartending shift would start. He kissed her cheek. "Ah. You're wearing the earrings." They were silver, with black stones to match Susan's raven hair.

"I like them. I've been wearing them a lot, or hadn't you noticed?"

"They remind me. I'm in sort of an ethical bind."

"About the earrings? Why, sweetie? Did you steal them for me?" She took flour out of the cupboard.

"No. It's something much trickier than that."

"I'm listening." She mixed salt, pepper, and flour together in a bowl.

"There's this guy who comes into the bar Monday nights during football season. Mick. And last year, after the last Monday game of the season, he stays until closing. He kind of buttonholes me, which is okay because there aren't more than a couple of other customers, and they're on their way out. He talks and talks about how good his life is, but there's this one thing he can't decide, and he wants to leave it up to me. He says 'The blonde, or the brunette?'"

Susan coated the chicken thighs in the flour mixture. "Meaning?"

"He had been dating these two women, and he liked them both. He figured that if he asked, either one would marry him. He couldn't make up his mind which one to ask."

"And you said?"

"Well, I told him I didn't have an opinion. I didn't know the women. I didn't really know him. But he said that made me impartial, and he wanted my answer anyway. So I said blonde."

Susan stopped flouring the chicken. "Blonde," she said.

"I could just have easily said brunette."

"But you didn't."

"I was just trying to tell him something that would end the conversation and send him on his way. It was time to close. I wanted to come home and climb into bed next to you. I didn't think it mattered what I said."

"If it didn't matter," she said, going back to work on the chicken thighs, "why didn't you say brunette?"

"That's not even the story, Babe. See, he didn't come in again until the next football season. So it's been maybe eight months. And when he sees me, it's like I'm his long-lost brother. He keeps telling everybody they should ask me for advice because the advice I give, it's primo. He has never been happier in his life."

"So did he leave a good tip?"

"Yeah, but it gets better. The next week, he has an envelope for me. 'Your consulting fee,'" he says. Inside I find $270 in crisp bills. And this is at the start of the evening, when he's stone cold sober. I tell him I think he's a little crazy. I have no problem keeping the money, though."

"If he'd go $270, why not $300?" Susan said. "Two-hundred and fifty would be more of a round number. What's the extra twenty for? Or why is thirty missing?" Chicken sizzles in the pan.

"Like I'd have any idea? I never laid eyes on his new wife. Anyway, that's where the money for your earrings came from. It came out of my $270 consulting fee. But that's not the end of it. This week, I could tell he had been drinking already even before he came in to the bar. He didn't say anything at all to me other than to order his first two rounds. So, later, when his glass is almost empty, I ask if he wants anything else. He says, 'I want my money back.' He wants me to repay the consulting fee. At first I said, 'No way.' But he said, 'Come on. You know you didn't really earn it.' And he's right. I mean, he could have flipped a coin. I just made a fifty-fifty choice for him."

"And you told him to marry the blonde."

"I told him I had spent the money. But he said it wasn't right for me to take advantage of him. Then I suggested half. I think I might pay back half."

Susan took the earrings off and put them on the counter. "Get whatever you can for these," she said.

"But you really liked them."

"Not so much. Get what you can, and then come up with the rest. Pay him back the full amount."

"With what? Susan, I won't get what I paid for the earrings. I have another tuition payment due next month. We can't afford this."

"We'll make do. It's like the man said. You didn't earn that money."

Ed bit his lip. "I guess."

"I'd feel differently," Susan said, "if you'd given him the right advice."

THREE:
THE SEVEN DEADLY HOTELS

Das Gästehaus der Schlafenziege

From the moment that I stepped from the white heat of noon into the shadows of the lobby, there were three members of the staff attending me. "Good day, Herr Doktor," said the first bellman, taking my valise. Ordinarily, I make a point of managing my own bags, but my walk up the long alleys and stairways from the train station had made me sweat. Mindful of my status, I had worn too many clothes, but really I could have dressed for comfort. I had met no one from the institute during my hike from the train to the Gästehaus. For good or for ill, none of my professional hosts were present to appreciate how I had overheated myself for the sake of appearances. I let the man take my bag, and when his assistant tried to pull my instrument case from my other hand, I resisted for only a moment.

"Be careful," I said. "Those are delicate medical devices."

"Of course," he said. He set the case onto a trolley. "We will take the utmost care, Herr Doktor."

"Herr Doktor, will you sit down?" said the woman. She lifted the hat from my head, a gesture far too intimate, but as she waved a fan and created a delightful breeze for my forehead, I could not protest. I closed my eyes. The bellmen, having deposited my things on the trolley, now gently pushed me back. I felt a chair at the back of my knees. As I sank into it, I could not repress a sigh. A kitchen servant curtsied as she presented me with an iced drink. "Will you take some lemonade, Herr Doktor?"

I allowed myself one sip, then said, "Perhaps I should go to the registration desk before I get too terribly comfortable." I tugged at the knot in my tie.

"Nonsense, Herr Doktor," said the woman who had taken my hat. "Registration will come to you. Now, if you will allow me..." She gave the fan over to one of the bellmen. Then I felt her slender fingers working to loosen my tie. She even unfastened the top button of my shirt. Again, such unwarranted intimacy! Yet the pleasure of unrestricted breathing curtailed my impulse to take umbrage.

"If you will sign, please, Herr Doktor," said a clerk kneeling before me.

"I must say," I told him, "I am quite surprised that you all should know who I am." I signed.

"We have so few vacancies at Das Gästehause der Schlafenziege," said the clerk. "You are our only new guest today."

"Really? I should have thought the hotels would be full of medical men arriving for the meeting."

"But we had only the one vacancy," said the clerk, smiling. "Only the one." The bellman still fanned cooling breezes toward my brow. The woman who had taken my hat, loosened my tie, and unfastened a button now kneaded the muscles in my neck just below my scalp. I opened my mouth to tell her to cease touching me at once, but I felt the muscles at my temples and the crown of my head relax as they had not relaxed in years. My jaw hung. I groaned. "To your room, then?" said the clerk.

"Ngh," I said, meaning to say that I would stand in just another moment.

The clerk apparently took my meaning. "No need to exert yourself," he said, and I discovered then that the chair had wheels.

As the bellmen pushed me through dim corridors, I half dozed. In my room, a fountain trickled. There is no soporific like the sound of moving water. My journey had taken more from me than I had realized. I had meant to visit the institute in the afternoon, but as my presentation was not until morning, I could wait. For now, sleep, or the cool relaxation just short of sleep, called to me.

The bellmen were valets as well. They began to undress me, and though I thought this strange and wrong, I did not want to halt the sensations of being touched, cared for. I knew how the purposeful and professional touch of my examinations could relax patients, but I received little contact of that sort myself. In my surgery, I saw much suffering. Was I not owed some pleasure by now, some freedom from care?

The valets helped me into bed. A gentle *tap-tap-tap* sounded at the door, and the valets admitted the woman whose touch I had never quite managed to protest when she had undone my tie. I did not protest now as she wrung a cloth into a basin and wiped the road dirt from my face, the remaining heat from my brow. I closed my eyes. She washed my arms, lifting them as if I were a paralytic. I let her. I let her wash my calves and feet. A valet stood at the side of the bed and slowly waved a large fan along the length of my body.

"Window," I mumbled. "Air." I always wanted fresh air as I slept. I heard the heavy draperies moved aside, heard the creak of the window hinges. Street noises drifted in.

I intended to give instructions, before the servants left me, for the hour at which I was to be wakened, but I couldn't rouse myself enough. I imagined speaking the necessary sentences, but I waited before speaking so as to enjoy the next moment, and the next. Then the hotel staff left me.

I dozed. I dreamed of sleeping on and on. I dreamed of people entering my room to feed me, to bathe me, to soothe me if ever I began to bestir myself. I dreamed of light behind the draperies, and darkness, and light again. Once I awoke to hear shouted voices in the street. The room was black. Glass broke. A shout. The sound of boots on cobbles, someone running away. Another shout, this time with words I understood. "Help! Help him! Doctor! Is there a doctor!"

I am a doctor, I thought. I imagined getting up, throwing on some clothes, and making my way out of the hotel. Such a bother. And when I found myself on the street, kneeling beside some man who no doubt had been complicit in his injury, would I remember what to do? I didn't think I would. I closed my eyes. I drowsed. I dozed. I dreamed of floating on warm water, floating farther away, farther away, farther.

The Hotel Ginger Plum

Once again I unburdened myself and unfolded the map to check my bearings, though this was difficult as the names of the streets were not posted at the intersection. Glancing to the right, to the left, and again straight ahead, I noticed a small boy standing before the great glass front of the next building. I could not tell what sort of establishment he might be staring into, but he gazed transfixed, in awe. I saw no signboard with the name of my destination or any other hotel or place of business. Still unsure of where I was, thinking that perhaps I should take the street to my right, I instead took up my baggage and advanced toward the boy to satisfy my curiosity about what he saw.

He was looking into a large room where richly upholstered chairs clustered around low tables. On each table were little baskets of tiny cakes and candies, and people sat in twos or threes at a few of these tables, tasting. Deeper inside, across a marble floor, stood a reception desk, and above this was a sign: *The Hotel Ginger Plum.* I had found the very place I sought! Feeling grateful to the boy for having served as my unwitting guide, I felt in my pocket for some coins and said, "Those sweets look very nice, don't they?"

He did not look away from the nearest basket, but only pressed his forehead against the glass.

"Look here," I said. "Why don't you go to a bakery or sweet shop and pick out something you like?" I held out the coins.

He did not look at me or at the proffered money. "You can't buy those," he said. "Those are only for guests."

"I'm sure you can get something nice." I jingled the coins.

He stood stock still. I had to lift up his hand for him and close his fingers around the coins. He did not thank me, but only continued to stare at the little basket. I began to wonder if, perhaps, he was not quite right.

The doorman admitted me, scowling at the boy as he did so. I checked in, ignoring the candy dish that was kept by the register. I rode the elevator to my floor. The corridor was cluttered with room-service dishes that had not been taken away, and I hurried past. In my room, I found a generous bowl of fruit on the bed table. The fruit was of the most ordinary assortment I could imagine – two apples, a banana, two oranges, and a pear. I was grateful for its simplicity. I was trying to lose weight, and perhaps if I satisfied myself with a piece of fruit, maybe the very blandest banana, I could do without dinner. In the morning I could have another piece of fruit and avoid the temptations of the breakfast room before my departure.

That was my plan, to eat only the banana, and perhaps an apple in the morning. But oh, what a banana it was! It looked like any banana I might have eaten before, with its slightly spotted skin. But the aroma as I peeled it was enchanting, with notes of apple, mango, and a delicate floral scent. As I bit into the fruit, I was astounded by the complexity of its foretaste, its delicate sweetness, the hint of tartness as my teeth crushed the yielding flesh. I chewed. As I swallowed, my mouth watered in anticipation of the next bite even as I detected a fading, volatile after-note.

When the banana was gone, I regretted that there had been only one. What a banana! I considered whether there would be any harm in trying one of the apples. I was eating fruit. Only fruit. Eating a meal of fruit was the very soul of moderation.

The apple was as novel and as glorious as the banana had been. Crisp, intense in both its tartness and its sweetness. Aromatic. When, I wondered, would I ever encounter another apple like that? Quite possibly never, unless the other one in the bowl was its equal, which it was. The oranges, likewise, were exquisite, and the pear. I called room service to ask if I might order a second bowl of fruit. After all, I would need a piece of fruit for my breakfast, and they sent up a larger bowl immediately with a complimentary basket of bread, which was the most extraordinary bread I had ever tasted. Also, a complimentary tureen of soup and a dense little pudding with custard sauce.

If only everything had been more ordinary, I would not have eaten it all. As I decided whether or not to eat the apple core, room service knocked on my door again. I hadn't ordered anything further. "Are you sure?" said the waiter, uncovering the plate of roasted lamb glazed in balsamic vinegar mint sauce with a side of buttered parsnips. "This isn't yours? Why don't you take it anyway? It would be a pity to have it go to waste. When will you ever have the chance to taste this particular preparation again? No charge."

I might have been able to say no, had I not smelled the

dish. But when, indeed, would I have a chance like this again? And while I washed my face in the bathroom, the maid let herself into my room, turned down the bed covers, and left the most exquisite mint on my pillow. After I had eaten it, I thought of the dish of candy at reception, and went down in my bathrobe just to have a look. There I discovered that the candies were custom made for the Hotel Ginger Plum. They were wrapped in seven different colors, and each flavor was like nothing I had ever tasted before, and when would I get to taste them again? On the tables in the lobby were those irresistible cakes and biscuits in the little baskets. I put some in my other pocket, the one that was not already full of candies, then ate most of them on my way back to my room. There were two waiters wheeling room service carts, stopping at the rooms of other guests where empty plates were already stacked outside the doors. In my absence, the maid had come again and put another mint on my pillow.

I was up most of the night eating. Although I had left no wake-up call, the phone rang early. It was the concierge reminding me that the breakfast room was now open. He began to describe the sweets and savories on offer.

Near noon, as I was checking out, I happened to turn from the front desk toward the street where I saw the boy again. He was standing in the same place as before, looking in at the nearest basket of complimentary sweets. I finished paying my bill. Then, supposing that I remained a guest of the hotel until I left the premises, I sat down at the table near the window and examined the contents of the basket. The boy watched as I ate lavender-colored cakes, pistachio-powdered biscuits, and little horns of flavored cream so scrumptious that I could not resist going around the lobby, from basket to basket, eating every last one of them.

Le Manoir Crapaud d'Or

My guide book advised me to pack light: "The climb from the roadway to the summit is challenging, and difficult to negotiate with heavy or oversized bags." As the taxi driver left me at the foot of the trail, I gazed up at the pinnacle of rock before me and decided that the guide book's caution was a marvel of understatement. As I had seen from miles away in the approaching cab, the sides of the salient were sheer and bare of vegetation except for a scraggly bush or stunted tree rooted here or there in a crack. I had packed light, with only one small suitcase. But even this seemed imprudent to me now, and I paused long enough to sort through my belongings and lighten my load. I cached my electric shaver, my pyjamas, one of my shirts and my book among some loose rocks and marked the location with a little pile of stones. Then I started up the trail.

Along with glossing over the hazards of reaching Le Manoir Crapaud d'Or, the guide book had failed to describe the beauty of the view. As I toted my little bag higher and higher above the valley floor, the forests and circling mountains presented me with an ever more breathtaking panorama.

The path itself was in most places wide enough for two travellers to pass, but I was nevertheless grateful not to encounter anyone else during my ascent. Along some of the wider stretches, a low curb of stones edged the path, but when the path narrowed and the edge dropped off abruptly, it was all I could do to resist the urge to drop to my knees and crawl. Crawling would be too slow. The sun was near the horizon, and I didn't know how much farther I had to climb.

I stopped briefly now and then to rest. Along the path, scraps of fabric hung here or there from snags of jagged rock or were tangled in the occasional stunted tree. Why, I wondered, would anyone want to mark the trail with strips of cloth?

As the sun continued to sink, I pressed on. At last, knees shaking, I stepped onto the level ground of the summit. The sun had dropped behind the mountains, though the sky was still blue. Le Manoir Crapaud d'Or, built from stone quarried from the pinnacle, rose before me like an enchanted palace, golden light spilling from every window.

I staggered into the foyer, collapsed in a chair, and was instantly attended by three members of the staff. A woman handed me a glass of champagne. "Not everyone who makes a reservation has the fortitude to arrive," she told me. She pointed out that the champagne flute was engraved with the name of the hotel and said that I was welcome to keep it as a remembrance. The little collection of amuses-bouche were likewise served on a souvenir plate, a piece of fine china bearing the name of the hotel and edged in gold.. Another woman wafted a cool breeze over my head with an ornamental fan. When I finally felt able to regain my feet and go sign the guest register, she folded the fan. "A memento," she said, presenting it to me.

Ordinarily, I would not have considered these objects worth keeping. Why bother with a champagne glass and plate that matched nothing else I owned? When would I ever use the fan again? But the ordeal of the trail infused these objects with significance. I had earned them. Not everyone who makes a reservation has the fortitude to arrive.

In my room, I discovered a pair of pyjamas laid out on the bed with a note explaining that if I wished to keep them, I could do so with the compliments of the hotel. They were silk, and dyed a deep blue that suits me very well.

I had dinner in the restaurant. The prices were nothing extraordinary. I resisted the waiter's suggestion that I could keep my entire place setting. The silverware alone would have been worth more than what I paid for the meal, and his generosity made me uneasy. I did accept the gift of the unique glass in which I was served my complimentary aperitif. The waiter asked, as he brought the check, if there was any object in the room that I fancied as a keepsake. Anything at all! I told him that really I was the sort of person who valued experiences rather more than objects.

Upon returning to my room I called the front desk to confirm the rate that I was paying for my room. It was hard to see how they could profit from my visit if I walked off with the silverware. What was the catch?

The wind had come up while I dined. Shutters rattled in the window frames of my room. After I had put on my silk pyjamas and slippers—all mine to keep—I remembered that I had left my book at the foot of the trail. I went down to the desk to ask if there were anything that I might borrow, and the clerk showed me into the library. I do not know what I expected as I began to survey the shelves. Outdated encyclopedias? Guidebooks left by previous guests? Tattered paperback novels? But the first title to catch my eye was a faded cloth cover stamped *Die Traumdeutung*. It looked old. Reverently I drew this treasure from its shelf, opened the spotless cover, and there beheld on the title page, below "von Dr. Sigm. Freud" and in well-aged ink, the signature of the author. "First edition?" I said. "Signed? My God! Do you realize what you have here?

"No one reads these," said the clerk. "If you see something you'd like to take home with you, feel free." He closed the door on his way out.

I could scarcely believe the other titles. *Ulysses* in the 1922 edition from Shakespeare & Company. Not signed. That would have been too much to hope for. But an actual first edition! There were some books I had never heard of by authors I hadn't read, but among the English titles I also found *The Hound of the Baskervilles, The Sun Also Rises,* and *The Sound and the Fury.* All first editions! Among the books in French, there were many that I didn't recognize, and some covers that were too old to read. I had to turn to title pages. My hands trembled when I found I was holding *Pensées de M. Pascal sur la religion.* I could not tell whether it was a first edition, but I read enough to determine that it was an early and uncensored one.

I carried a stack of books to reception. "Some of these," I said, "are almost certainly worth a great deal of money. Are you sure that I may have them?"

"Sir," he said. He paused as a gust of wind shook the doors and shutters. "Sir, help yourself to anything that pleases you.

Anything at all. Except for the linens. If you want any bed or bath linens, you have to pay for them."

I hauled the stack to my room and returned to the library for more. I made two more trips to the library. Three. Four. My hoard consisted of more books than I could possibly carry. I went to the desk again. "Is it possible to hire someone to carry my things down for me in the morning?"

He gave me a disapproving look. "It is entirely out of the question."

In my room, I fell into a fever of sorting. I would not keep the souvenir plate or the champagne flute. Well, perhaps the champagne flute, as I could wrap it in the pyjamas. I had earned it. Could I discard some of my clothes? But even if I carried nothing but books in my little suitcase, there would be books that would not fit, books that I could not bear to leave behind.

I returned to the desk. "Could I leave some things here and come back for them another time?"

"Sir," said the clerk, "what do you think we are? The Manoir offers you its hospitality, but we are not a warehouse."

I could perhaps tie books into a bundle made from the pyjamas. But what if the books spilled out on the trail? The sheer silk might split at the seams. What I needed was another suitcase or a backpack or...

"The pillowcases," I said. "How much?"

The clerk reached under the counter and brought out the price list. I blinked and made sure that the numbers were what they seemed. "For pillowcases?" I said.

He nodded. "We accept credit cards, of course."

Now I could see where Le Manoir Crapaud d'Or made its profit. The pillow cases cost as much as what I imagined a pillowcase full of first-edition books would be worth. Even so, it wasn't about the money. It was about leaving with no regrets. How could I live with myself if I left behind such treasure?

All night, as the the wind howled around the hotel, I sorted and resorted my books, my lovely books and considered whether, instead of pillow cases, I really ought to go with a sheet.

Pensiunea Calul Bălan

I didn't much like the look of the two hotels on the main street, each with worn carpets, interchangeably bored desk clerks, and a lobby reeking of stale tobacco, so despite the lateness of the hour I shouldered my little bag and made my way into the winding cobblestoned side streets. Most windows were dark. I found a restaurant, closed, and a drinking establishment whose sole patron eyed me with bleary contempt.

I resigned myself to choosing the less shabby of the two hotels, if I could determine which one that was, but now I was lost. The curving streets brought me into a little square, and there, by moonlight, I saw a sign bearing the figure of a white horse, and below that, in big letters I could just make out, *PENSIUNEA*.

Dim light showed in one of the windows. I tried the locked door, then knocked. I thought I heard the creak of a floorboard, but even my second knock brought no answer. Just as I turned to go, lantern light moved in the space between the pension and the house next to it. The gate opened, and the elderly man who appeared there lifted the lantern high so that we gazed into one another's faces by its light. He smiled.

"*Bună seara,*" I said. "Do you have a room for the night?"

He smiled more broadly. "Not for just anyone," he said. "But for you, certainly!" He knocked on the locked door twice, once, then twice again, and the door opened from within. I was admitted to a fire-lit sitting room by a lovely woman—his daughter, I supposed.

She said, "You are to be congratulated. Not everyone who looks is able to find us."

The man added, "Not everyone who finds us is admitted. But for someone of your stature..." He waved his hand.

"Someone of my stature?" I said. What could these people in a remote town know of me? Although I have a considerable reputation in some circles, surely that reputation was not the sort that could precede me.

"Someone," said the woman, "of your tastes. One needs only to look at how you dress. We don't open for just anyone, you know. Oh, no! Most certainly not!"

"*Domnişoara*," I said politely, "I give hardly any thought to my clothes."

"Obviously," she said, "you care for greater refinements than mere appearance. And you have troubled yourself to learn our language!"

"Only a few words."

"That raises you above the common sort of traveller," said the man. I smiled at that. I do think it matters that I learn a few polite words wherever I go. He said, "Shall I show you a room, then?"

We climbed the stairs, he and I, to a cozy, tidy bedroom. The furnishings were dark and sturdy. "This will do nicely," I said.

"Yes," he agreed, "this is a suitable for our most ordinary class of guest."

"So there's something better?"

"It costs a little more. But, yes, there is something better, for guests of a more discerning taste. But, after all, once you are asleep, what does it matter what the room looks like, eh? This will suit you, then?"

"Well," I said, "perhaps you could show me the other room?"

He smiled. "I knew you weren't of that ordinary class. Mind you, all of our guests are a cut above, but I did think you were the sort who, well, you'll see!"

I followed him up another flight of stairs. From a utilitarian perspective, this second room was the same size as the first, was equipped with a bed, a dresser, a desk and two chairs. But every piece of furniture was embellished with delicate carvings, and the paintings on the wall were well-executed landscapes. "Lovely!"

"Yes, lovely. Yes." He nodded. "You like it, then? It's a suitable room for an art lover with mundane tastes. Is this where I should settle you?"

"I'm not sure," I said. I felt a little insulted. My tastes were hardly limited to the mundane.

"Well, there is the next room upstairs," he said, "but it's really for our thoroughly modern guests. The furnishings are, you see, rather avant garde. And it costs rather a lot more. It might be beyond your means, and at your age..."

At my age, he said! At my age! I was not nearly as old as he was! I was not so many years older than his pretty daughter, in fact, or at least not so much older that, well, that she would ever say to me, as she surely said to him: *At your age...*

"I want to see this room. Show it to me!"

"Very well." He led the way up the stairs. When I saw the room, I had to laugh for two reasons. The first was that the furnishings were not so very avant garde as he thought. They were sleek, Danish modernist pieces, and the table was not unlike one that I had at home. The paintings on the wall were handsome oils depicting figures in modern dress in classic poses amid allegorical settings. Brilliant stuff, really, and the sort of thing that not everyone is able to appreciate. I said so. I said that the room and the price suited me very well. I dropped my bag on the bed.

"I must say," the old man said, "that I had not recognized you as such a connoisseur. I congratulate you for your taste and your persistence. Breakfast is in the sitting room. Now, unless you need anything else, I will say good night."

"Just a moment," I said. I put my hands on my hips. "Is there yet another room?"

He turned away. "Not for a man in your condition," he said.

"What?" I said. "A man in my what?"

He looked over his shoulder at me. "I mean nothing by it. You're a man who has lived some already, yes?" He turned to face me. "We know that you're a man of the world, a man who appreciates fine things. But lets be honest, sir. Refined taste takes time to acquire. You're no young stallion any longer, no more than I am. The only remaining room is suitable, frankly, for an athlete, a man in his prime. In fact, it was made specifically for an athlete in his twenties."

I retrieved my bag. "I would like to see this room."

"I will show it to you, but you must understand that I can't let you stay there. I couldn't be responsible for what might happen."

"Lead the way," I said.

We passed through what seemed to be the attic, through a hatch in the roof, and up another set of stairs into a still higher moonlit structure on stilts. Within that structure, we came to a landing before a locked door. Next to the door was a great two-handled lever of the sort found attached to water pumps in mines. "We have to raise the floor to enter," the old man said. He took hold of the lever at one end and directed me to the handle opposite. As we worked the lever, the landing vibrated with the rattling of chains taking up slack beneath us, and then the squeak of machinery and the groan of great beams. At last came a loud *BANG!* "It's set for ten minutes now," he said. "It won't last longer than that without working the machines. We mustn't linger." He unlocked the door.

The attic room inside was Spartan. There was a bed. Next to that, a table, and mounted on the table an alarm clock. The old man wound and set the clock, showing me as he did so that the clock was solidly attached to the table, and that the table was nailed to the floor. The bed, too, was nailed down, the bare mattress strapped to the frame. "When the room is at rest," the old man explained, "this floor swings open. Anyone inside would be flung to the roof or the street below."

"Why?" I said. "For what possible purpose...?"

"Built for a much younger man," the proprietor explained. "A man devoted to his strength, his endurance. These apparatus..." He went to one of the four corners. He took the handle of the machine there and demonstrated the action. "This one strengthens the arms." He went to another corner. "This one, the legs." He crossed to the third. "You must pardon the nature of this demonstration. You did ask to see this room." The third machine required a vigorous thrusting of the hips. The sexual application of the motion required no imagination. The fourth machine similarly prepared the body for extensive carnal labor. "These machines, like the handles outside, work the mechanism that keeps the floor upright. By means of vigorous work, a man can build up the mechanical energy to hold the floor in position for up to an hour at a time. But then he must rise and do it all again. Or else."

"This is crazy!" I said. "Who would submit himself to such torture?"

"A man not at all like you or I," said the proprietor. "A man of youthful vigor, of legendary stamina. A man for whom the very building of this room enhanced his reputation for scandal. But for us, such days are over, are they not? If ever we knew such days at all?" He laughed. I did not laugh with him. I was realizing that once he left me for the night, his daughter would certainly ask him which room I had chosen. What sort of knowing smile might she have for a man who at my age, yes, at my age, had stayed the night in the top-most room?

When the old man saw my expression, he insisted upon cash payment in advance.

Grønn Hotell

While I waited for the crew of the freighter to fetch the steamer trunks from my cabin, a hotel agent roaming the dock approached to make me an offer that seemed too good to be true. The handbill from the Grønn Hotell featured engraved illustrations of a plain, simple room with only a bed, a table, and a chair—all at a reasonable price. But beneath this illustration were engravings of a much finer room with a bigger bed, elegant furnishings, and a splendid view over the village and down to the sea. Additional images showed a vast courtyard with a swimming pool, steam room, and a bar.

These additional amenities, explained the agent, were available at no extra cost to any guest who paid for a basic room. I thought at first that I had misunderstood him, and that the extras were for those paying for a fancy room. But the agent said, no, the extras were for anyone. Anyone who paid for a basic room could use a grander room at no charge. Anyone who paid for a basic room might swim in the pool for free. Anyone who paid for a basic room could have a few drinks at the bar without paying a single *øre* more. Meals in the dining room? No extra cost. Next I wondered at the value of the local money. Had I erred in calculating the exchange rate?

"Please do not worry, sir," he said. "Everything is as I say."

I agreed to have a look at the place, anyway. He waved a green flag high in the air, and a motorcar turned onto the dock and made slow progress toward us among the departing sailors and the longshoremen at work. The agent and driver loaded my trunks into the car, and then the driver steered the car slowly off the dock, through the village, and up the side of the mountain. The road to the Grønn Hotell wove up the side of the slope, this way and that, providing a view of at least two sides of the hotel. It was big, but I already knew that it surrounded a large courtyard. Strangely, only the topmost floor had windows looking outward with a view to the village, the sea, the islands, or the surrounding slopes. The lower floors all presented a blind face of solid brick. Without windows to count, it was impossible to know how high the building might be. Seven stories? Eight? And if the guest rooms were all on the top, what was the purpose of the lower floors?

At the reception desk, in frames, there were the same engravings that I had already seen of the basic room. Then, the extras: The swimming pool. The steam room. The dining hall. The bar. The better, optional room with a grand view. I tapped the illustration of the better room. "All included?" I asked the clerk.

"Everything is included," he said.

I wanted to see one of these grander rooms. The clerk said that such rooms were exclusive to the top floor. He gave me a key and showed me to the stairs. Eight flights up, I stepped into a thickly carpeted silent corridor where gas lights burned outside of each brass-appointed door. I let myself into a room. The engraving had not done the place justice. The furnishings were elegant and clean. I opened a window and inhaled the scents of pine from the mountains and salt from the sea. Sunlight glittered on the distant harbor.

As I descended the stairs, I was already counting out my money. What a bargain!

"There is just one thing more to understand about the hotel," the clerk said when I laid my money on the counter. "You enjoy the optional amenities at the pleasure of the other guests. If another guest wishes to deny you any amenity beyond the basic room, he or she may do so for a fee." He laid a price list on the counter. "And you, of course, may deny other guests in the same way, if you choose."

Again, I wondered if I had misunderstood. But the price list seemed clear enough, in five languages: Deny better room. Deny dining hall. Deny bar. Deny swimming. Deny steam. Each with a price.

Well, I thought, what could this have to do with me? Why should any other guest care about the room that I stay in or the pleasures that I enjoy?

"By paying the basic room price," said the clerk, "you agree to abide by this condition."

"I suppose," I said with a shrug. "I want one of those rooms like the one that I just saw. On the top floor."

"Certainly, sir."

"They aren't already taken?"

"Not at all, sir."

I signed. The clerk rang for the bellman, who had already loaded my trunks onto a trolley. We did not take the stairs. From the carpeted lobby, we exited into the courtyard where the trolley's metal wheels clattered against the paving stones.

The sound echoed among all the inward looking windows of the rooms on lower floors. These were, I supposed, the basic rooms. I hadn't even asked to inspect one. Well, I wasn't going to stay in one of those places, with their courtyard-facing windows. Not when I could have a grand room with a wonderful view.

All the way across the courtyard, past the pool and entrance for the steamroom, a glass lift awaited. The bellman opened the lift doors, stowed my trunks inside, and then went around the outside of the car fitting green flags into sconces.

"What are the flags for?" I said.

He shrugged, which I took to mean that he spoke no English. He closed the door and turned the crank on the lift telephone a few times. He held the earpiece as he said a few words into the receiver. Across the courtyard, a whistle sounded. So much procedure for running the elevator up! So much pomp and theater! At last the bellman pulled the lever to start our creaking ascent. As we rose, I decided that the flags made the ride in the lift more festive. And I was, after all, on my way to the top floor, the realm of special luxury! I looked across the courtyard at the windows of the basic rooms. The curtains of each window were parted a little. How fortunate I was that there was space in the better rooms, simply for the asking! I thought I saw the curtains in one room move. And in another room, the curtains most certainly stirred. Poor souls, stuck in a basic room. Yes, I was most fortunate indeed.

We were still some distance from the top when the bells on the telephone jangled. The bellman halted the lift, lifted the earpiece, and listened in silence. He replaced the earpiece, and we descended to the courtyard. He wheeled my trunks out of the elevator. "Come," he said. He removed the green flags from the lift.

"My room," I said, "is up there. Top floor." I motioned with my hands: Up! Up!

"Room," he said, nodding. I followed him across the courtyard, down a corridor, and into the cage of a much less refined lift. We arrived at the fourth floor where he showed me to a room. A basic room. It was even dingier than the engravings had made it look: a narrow bed, a table next to the parted curtains, a chair. On the table were a pair of binoculars and a sheet of paper.

"No, no," I said. "I want a room on the top floor."

"Room," he said. He lingered in the doorway as if I might tip him. Most certainly not! Instead, I followed him back to the ground floor.

I said to the clerk, "Now see here! I'm entitled to one of the rooms on the top floor!"

"Sir," said the clerk, "you paid for a basic room. You requested a better room, but another guest paid to deny you the top floor."

"Well in heaven's name, why would anyone do that? I don't know anyone here! I've never even been to this country before today!"

"I'm very sorry," said the clerk. "But you still have the basic room. It's a good value. You have the other amenities..."

"Someone actually paid money to keep me from enjoying the better room? Who?"

The clerk only shook his head.

I considered returning to my room, but the sight of it would only make me angry. I went to the bar. The gaslights burned low. The place was full. Angry faces turned toward me from every table, and I glared back. No one had better deny me this amenity, I thought. I ordered a whisky and soda, and then another, quick, before someone ruined my chance. A man and woman came in together, laughing, and someone at the bar shoved money across to the bartender and spoke a few words in a low voice. When the laughing man approached the bar and said, "We'll have...," the bartender shook his head.

"Not for you," he told them.

"What do you mean?" the man said, not laughing now.

Join the club, I thought.

I had another drink. No one denied me. I tried not to look as if I were enjoying it.

Back in my basic room, I sat heavily in the chair before the table. The sheet of paper, I discovered, was the price list. Deny, deny, deny, in five languages.I picked up the binoculars and gazed through the parted curtains into the courtyard. The glass car of the lift was empty, but there was a family of fat people walking across the paving stones dressed in bathing costumes. Their forearms and calves were pink. The man had a full moustache. I have never been able to grow a moustache like that, damn him. I turned the focus ring to see him better. He smiled as he dipped his toes in the water. His wife smiled. The children looked content. Their mouths were open, and they might all have been laughing as they waded into the pool.

I examined the price list again. How much to deny swimming?

L'Hotel Fiasco Rosso

I arrived long after midnight, exhausted. The wide front window of L'Hotel Fiasco Rosso was painted with the establishment's emblem, a red flask tipped to pour its contents. As I stepped from my cab, I tried to get a look at the lobby through that window, but I couldn't see past the shelves displaying all manner of porcelain and crystal—cups, saucers, wineglasses and figurines. If "Hotel" weren't part of the name, I'd have thought I was standing in front of a china shop. The bellman—an old man with white hair —started to move my luggage from the cab and onto a trolley. "Go on ahead, sir," he said, resting with his hands on his knees after he had shifted the first bag. "I'll be along."

The window display of glass and china provided a good foretaste of the lobby. There were glass shelves along all the walls, among the lobby furniture, and behind the front desk. All of these shelves and all of the low tables held china or bric-à-brac. The desk itself was cluttered end to end with figurines and teacups, each one sporting a little paper price tag. Behind the counter was a boy who looked too young to possibly be the clerk, but as I approached, he asked if I had a reservation. I gave him my name. He looked at two sheets of paper in front of him and frowned. He asked me to say my name again. I did. He frowned again and asked me to spell it out. I did.

"This isn't you, is it?" Over the cluttered counter, he passed me a form with someone else's name.

"No."

"Not this one either?" The characters on this form weren't even in the right alphabet.

"Most certainly not."

"Oh." He picked up the telephone, then put it down when there was apparently no answer on the other end. "Well, you don't have a reservation," he said.

"But I do," I insisted.

"It's all right," he said. "I'll find you a room anyway. Passport?" I gave him my passport. He opened a notebook. The page he opened to looked to me like a confused mass of scribbled notes. He frowned, added a few pencil marks to the page, and then handed me a form to fill in. I took the form away because there was not enough space on the desk counter for me to fill it out there. But there wasn't space on any of the coffee tables in the lobby, either. Dishes and figurines covered every surface. Gingerly, I removed a tiny cow, a vase, a girl with an umbrella, a flowered cup and saucer, and two miniature buildings from an end table so I could have a hard writing surface. I noted the prices on the items as I handled them. They were nothing I would ever want to own, but someone valued them highly, it seemed. When I had filled in the form, I put the pieces back in their place.

I returned to the desk. I pointed to a space that the boy should have filled in. "And the rate?"

He quoted me an amount half again as much as what I had secured with my reservation. "That's wrong," I told him.

It was still a good price, better than any other quote I'd had for the city, but a deal's a deal. "That is not what I reserved."

"You didn't reserve anything," he said. "Don't try to fool me."

That was no way for him to talk to a customer, or to any adult, for that matter! I held my tongue, though. He was only a child. "Let me speak to someone else," I said. "The manager."

"They aren't answering," he said. "They never answer at this time of night." He picked up the phone, dialed, listened, then hung up. "See?"

"Well, then, I'll just have to sort this out in the morning. With someone responsible." I looked around. "Where's the bellman with my luggage?"

The boy opened a drawer and took out a piece of paper. "How many pieces?"

"What?"

He asked the question more slowly. "How. Many. Pieces? Of luggage? How many pieces of luggage are you claiming to have lost?"

"I haven't lost any. They're with the bellman."

"If you gave them to the bellman," said the boy, "they're lost."

As if to confirm this, the bellman entered the lobby then, pushing an empty trolley.

"You there!" I called out. I strode to the bellman. "What have you done with my bags!"

"Your bags, your bags," said the bellman, rubbing the back of his head. "So they were your bags, were they?"

"My bags," I said. "The ones you were just taking from the cab!"

"Were you coming or going?" he said. "Dear me."

I hurried out of the hotel onto the empty street. The cab was gone. There was no sign of my luggage. When I returned to the lobby, the bellman was nowhere in sight. The boy waited, holding up his lost-luggage form, and asked again, "How many pieces?"

When the elevator doors opened on the top floor, they opened onto cold darkness. I stepped out, thinking that perhaps the corridor lights would come on when I did. When the elevator doors closed behind me, it was very dark indeed. I groped forward, found a door, but I couldn't feel a number on it. I looked up and saw stars. The top floor had no roof. I groped my way back to the elevator, but nothing happened when I pressed the button. I had to find and take the stairs.

"You sent me to the roof!" I told the boy.

"Oh, right," he said. "No top floor right now. Because of the construction." He consulted his notebook again, then gave me a key for a room on another floor.

I found that room, but when I went to wash my face, there was no water.

The boy consulted his notebook. "I guess they turned the water off on that floor. Because of the construction." He gave me a third key.

In the third room, soiled sheets and bath linens were piled on the floor. The mattress was bare.

The boy spent a long time turning the pages of his

notebook this time, then told me that probably that room wasn't supposed to be used because of the construction. He gave me a fourth key. When I rode the elevator again, found the room, opened the door and turned on the light, I discovered that a couple was already in the bed. The man sat up. "Now what?" he said. "Who the hell are you?"

"Sorry," I said.

"Sorry, my ass! Get the hell out of our room!" He seized something from the bed table and threw it. The object shattered on the wall near my head. I shut the door. In my haste, I failed to turn out the light. "Asshole!" I heard him say. Well, none of this was my fault!

As I returned to the lobby, I pondered the question of just whose fault it was. The child at the desk wasn't old enough to be competent. The bellman was too senile to remember what he was doing. Who had hired them? What idiot of a manager was running this place?

"Well," said the boy when he gave me my fifth key of the night, "you should have made a reservation."

The bed in the fifth room was made. The lights worked. Water ran from the tap. The toilet flushed. There was no soap in the soap dish, only a ceramic imitation of a bar of soap. There were ceramic flowers on the cistern of the toilet. I rinsed my face, since I couldn't really wash it. I stripped to my underwear, since I had no pyjamas to wear. With care, I removed the expensive figurines from the night stand, afraid that I might knock them onto the floor in my sleep. I turned out the light, and got into bed.

Bang! Bang! Bang! Bang!

I sat up.

Bang! Bang!

It sounded as if someone were hammering the walls in the room next to me. I turned on the light, dialed the front desk, and the boy told me, "Yes, that's the construction. Do you want me to put you in a different room?"

"No," I said. "I'm coming down." I dressed. I returned to the lobby. "Give me my passport," I said. "I'm leaving."

"Not without paying, you aren't," the boy said.

"Give me my passport, you impudent runt!" I picked up a ballerina and snapped off her head. "Give me my passport, or so help me..."

"I can't!" he said. He started to cry. "I can't until you pay for the room!"

"God damn you!" I roared. I swept a dozen cups and figurines onto the floor where they landed with a satisfying smash.

He flinched at the sound. "And those," he said, wiping his cheeks with his sleeve, glaring at me with reddened eyes. "You'll have to pay for those, too."

El Hotel Mono Rojo

Some brothers of my order used the name of the city as another word for sin. They spoke in hushed voices of the fallen women, the boys for sale, the corrupting commerce of that place, and they worried for the soul of any man who went there. They worried for my soul in particular, and bade me farewell with promises of fervent prayers of protection. I was unafraid. Even as a younger man, when I still sometimes struggled with the temptations of the flesh, I had been the courier for our abbey. Our order made money from painting and selling icons. Twice a year for many years I had crossed the desert, stayed in the city, and continued the next day to deliver our surplus earnings to the convent school. On the way home, I would again spend the night in the city. The city always tried to tempt me, but repeating the words "The glory of God" had always protected me. I had never fallen.

This experience had persuaded me that I knew all the methods by which travellers were lured. Thus did I consider myself safe. Besides, I was an old man now, resigned to the impermanence of flesh and less impressed by the shape of a woman's calf or the swell of her breasts. When I entered the outskirts of the city, women called to passing men from shadowed doorways, but few of them bothered with me. My white hair, the simplicity of my robe and sandals, my resolute stride, or perhaps some other signal indicated I was a poor target. Had they known how much money I carried in my leather purse, they might have made more of an effort. But it still would have been in vain.

In the hotel district, I chose the lodging with a sign showing a red ape and the words "Hotel Mono Rojo." I had stayed here before. The hotels on this street were inexpensive, for the owners expected to make their money in other ways. From me, they had never collected more than the single coin for lodging.

In the lobby, every chair leg, every pillar, every carpentry joint where one piece of wood met another was shaped like a limb, like a woman striking an alluring pose, like a union of flesh with flesh. In the dark wooden panels of the walls lurked lines and shapes that suggested, but did not quite reveal, various acts of carnal knowledge among men, women, and perhaps…. But it was best not to speculate. The frankly erotic paintings were less dangerous, less of a lure to the imagination. "The glory of God," I whispered to myself. Wherever my gaze fell, there was temptation: in the carpet pattern of the red nymphs and black satyrs, or in the carmine fingernails of the clerk as she beckoned me closer to sign the register.

However, the lobby was the worst of it. I was soon ascending the stairs with the bellman, who held my key, though I had asked to carry it myself. My only burdens were the purse at my waist and a loaf of bread tied into a cloth. I needed no assistance. "Just let me show you the way, sir," he said.

He opened the door for me. When he did so, I caught sight of a feather lying on the floor. I stepped into the room and bent to pick the feather up. It was most unusual, with a golden shaft and a white vane edged in gold. The bellman snatched it out of my hand. "Very sorry, sir," he said. "You ought not to have seen that." He put the feather in his breast pocket.

"Why?" I said. "What is it?"

"I, I don't know how it got here. Sometimes the chamber maids are careless! Will that be all, sir?" He worked to stuff the feather ever deeper into his pocket in a manner that struck me as theatrical, as if by his actions he were saying, *Forget all about the feather,* but in a way designed to make me think of nothing else. I thought I understood, then. This was one of the ploys such establishments depended on. Well, I would not be taken in. "Yes," I said. "That is all. You may go, and good night to you."

He paused in the doorway. He turned to look at me and said, "Well if you must know, it is a feather from the angel."

I didn't reply. I imagined that this discovery of the feather and the bellman's stammering disavowal was a performance enacted with some regularity at El Hotel Mono Rojo. I was meant to say, *The Angel?* And the Angel would turn out to be some costumed dancer, the star of a cabaret or the object of an even more sinful entertainment. "Good night," I said again.

"I have only glimpsed it myself," the bellman said, still blocking the door. "No one knows why it doesn't fly back to heaven. And no one so far can understand its speech. But maybe you...."

So the angel was not a carnal temptation, but an invention used for some spiritual fraud. I still would not be taken in. "Bless you, my son," I insisted, "and good night!" I closed the door behind him and locked it.

An angel! In this place! Absurd!

I made my modest dinner of bread. While I chewed, a thought came to me: Why should there not be an angel in a place such as this? Is God not present even in the lives of sinners? Will his messengers not appear among the wicked, who have more need of divine messages than the pious?

I put these thoughts from my mind as I lay down to sleep. From the next room came the rhythmic *thump thump thump* and muffled cries of adulterous exertions. "The glory of God!" I chanted aloud. "The glory of God!"

What did I know, truly, of the glory of God? I prayed that one day my chastity and humility would be rewarded and I would know God's glory. But what if I need not wait until my last breath? "The glory of God" I whispered, as I tried to recall the details of the feather. Had it looked like an ordinary feather decorated by a clumsy hand? Or was it, indeed, an object of astonishing beauty?

Here is the nature of sin: I had doubts, of course, and yet I could not sleep for thinking of the angel. My prayer failed to bring serenity or sleep. Before dawn had broken, I found myself paying the grinning bellman, with money that was not even my own, and following him to the top floor into a little room hung with red curtains. When the curtains drew back to reveal a dim circular room with mirrors all around, mirrors that could only be the windows of other little curtained rooms, I knew the vice that this place ordinarily celebrated, the sorts of things that other guests must pay to witness. I knew all of this, yet when the curtain parted, I held my breath. I stared.

Though the light was dim, though reason told me that I must be seeing some trick of goose feathers, gold paint, and wax, I beheld the most graceful and beautiful creature that my eyes had ever seen. I saw an angel. I witnessed the gentle expansion of the wings as the angel breathed, the curve of its down-covered fingers. It had its winged back to me. How I longed to see its face! "The glory of God!" I whispered, filled with longing. "The glory of God!"

FOUR

Donat Bobet, Renunciate

Someone rang my apartment from the lobby. It was Donat Bobet. He said he must see me at once, and when I met him at my door, his expression was severe. "We live in an age of horrors," he said as he handed me an envelope. "The hour for renunciation is at hand."

"Donat," I said, "won't you come in? Take off your coat. What is this all about?"

But he would not enter. He held many more envelopes in his gloved hand. He had other deliveries to make. "Read," he said. "I hope to see you at the appointed time, my friend."

Inside the envelope was a sort of handbill:

➤MASS MURDER OF INNOCENTS◀

☞ ASSASSINATION ☜

✋STARVATION✋

💣❊CRUELTY💣❊

☠WAR☠

Humanity visits terrors upon its fellow man.
Humanity wreaks havoc upon the earth.

Humanity devours and does not replenish.
Enough, we say! Enough!
Not in our name!
On Thursday at 19:30, we will act!
Meet among the trees on the east side of the
Lac Aux Castors in the Parc Mont-Royal.
Bring your certification of humanity.
Come hungry

I was not sure just what my certification of humanity should look like. At a stationers, I bought some cream-colored parchment and gold seals, along with a special pen for calligraphy. Each day at work, I looked at my diploma and the framed documents of other workers for hints about how my certificate should read. "To All Who Shall See These Words, Greetings: Know Ye that the Universe, in the name and by the authority of Everything That Is has granted a human birth to the bearer herein named, and that he is accorded all the rights and responsibilities persuant to such a birth..." When I had settled upon a satisfactory draft, I carefully copied the words onto the parchment and affixed gold seals and a few ribbons.

I arrived at the park a little early and found people standing among the trees beside the frozen lake. It had been dark for hours by then, but the glow of city lights illuminated the clouds and the snowy ground. Children still sledded on the dark toboggan hill. It was light enough, in fact, that I could recognize a few of the other men and women who stood shivering with me. I had seen them at Bobet's parties or dining with him in cafés.

"Do you know what we are doing here?" I said to one man.

"You have brought your certificate?"

"Of course." I took mine from my breast pocket and showed it to him. There wasn't enough light to read by, but he could see the seals and ribbons. He said it was very fine and showed me his, which I must say was not quite as decorative as my own. "But what are we to do with them?"

"Ah," he said. "Here comes the poet. All will be revealed, I am sure."

Indeed, when Donat Bobet came through the trees to join us he said without preamble, "My friends, the night is cold, so let us proceed. I am ashamed of our species. Humanity is capable of so much good, yet the newspapers fill up every day with accounts of our wicked accomplishments. I have had enough!"

He produced a sheet of paper. "My own certification of humanity," he said. He took off one glove. In his bare hand, a white spark flashed. A flame. He was holding a cigarette lighter. "Humanity," he said, "I renounce you! I resolve from this night forward to be something more noble than a human being!" As he held the flame to a corner of his certificate, I could see the colored inks, the hand-drawn seals, the filigreed borders, and I thought it was a pity to set fire to one of his creations before any of us had even read it.

Flame devoured the paper. Bobet let go before the fire reached his fingers. Black ash and one glowing fragment of paper fell onto the snow.

"Who will join me?" He held up the lighter. One by one,

the others came forward with their certifications. One by one, they renounced humanity.

All but a few of us. I don't think it was pride that made me resist, though I did think I had made rather a handsome document. I said, "There is enough good in humanity that I think I will keep mine."

"A choice no less brave, no less daring, than the path of the renunciates," said Bobet. "I think that you cling to a corrupt species, but perhaps it is not too late to change it from within." He suggested that we proceed to Entrecôte St-Jean for dinner.

The brasserie was warm and crowded, with tables too close together. We were near McGill University, so as many customers shouted their conversations in English as in French. Entrecôte St-Jean had the shortest menu in Montreal. You were going to have walnut salad and steak in mustard sauce whether you liked it or not. Bobet ordered nothing for himself, but visited the plates of his guests, eating a few shoe-string potatoes here, a bite of steak there, half of a chocolate profiterole, then half of another, and half of a third. Before the check had come, he was saying, "Good night, my friends. Whatever I am now, whatever you have become, I bid you good night."

After he had gone, one woman said, "I wonder if tomorrow I will wake up and find that I have wings!"

"Tomorrow," said a man, "we may be invisible."

I had no hope of invisibility or wings. But I still had my handsome certificate.

I seldom thought again of that night. In the spring, I dropped in on the poet unannounced. I brought a bottle of wine and some cheese, sufficient to ensure that he would ask me in. I knocked. He was some time in opening his door.

"Donat!" I said. "Look at this Côte du Rhône that I found! Such a bargain! Naturally, I thought of you at once!" Then I noticed the redness of his eyes. His tears. "My friend, what is wrong?"

"Such are the trials of love," he said. "Come in. Come in." He relieved me of the wine and cheese. A young woman sat in his living room. Her face, too, was wet with tears. She dried them. "You remember Lisabette, of course?"

I had met her before. In this very room, when the poet had led us on an African safari, she had been the zebra. Months ago, she had been among those who had renounced their humanity in the park.

"You will think us sentimental, perhaps," said Bobet. "Lisabette has met a man. They intend to marry. But he has not renounced his humanity. He refuses."

"A mixed marriage," Lisabette explained. "The world will be against us."

"And there is the future to consider," added Bobet. "What will the child of such a union be like? Perhaps a monster? Or perhaps a being too delicate to exist in this world?"

At these words, Lisabette began to weep aloud. Bobet dabbed at his own eyes.

I laughed. "Come, now," I said. "You take this too far. Lisabette burned a scrap of paper in the park. What difference can this mean to her child?"

My words only made her weep all the more. Bobet gave me a stern look. Then he took the young woman's hands in his.

"Courage," he told her. "Lisabette, you must be brave. The terrors of bringing a child into this world are no different under your circumstances. Yes, it is awful to contemplate. But it is the same, my dear. It is the same."

About the Author

Early in life, the author demonstrated his facility with language when he began to speak fluent English without any formal instruction. To this day, he could learn any language with ease if he only cared to and applied himself a little. Prior to his full-time writing career, he held a wide variety of jobs, including third-shift line operator, second-shift line operator, first-shift line operator, third-shift deputy supervisor of line operations, and weekend pizza delivery guy.

The author wrote this book in six months, before his unemployment benefits ran out.

The author has been suggested as a finalist—or at least his name has almost certainly come up—for several literary honors, among them the Commendation for Pending Recognition, the Literary Use of Words Certificate of Eligibility, and the Citation Prize Award for Nominations.

The author started to write this book on a computer at the library, but found the conditions there both stultifying and distracting. He found that literary composition demanded the physicality of paper. When holding a pen in his hand, the author felt that he stood on the shoulders of literary giants, that he continued a noble tradition. For a time, it looked as if the author's car might be repossessed before he finished writing the manuscript.

The author is the author of several uncollected stories, some of which have very nearly appeared in *Thinkin' n Imaginin'* and *The Thrifty Nickel*, which, as it turns out, does not publish fiction. The same stories might have appeared in *The New Yorker, North American Review*, and *Paris Review*, had they been submitted and accepted.

The author feels that writing a first draft in a bound notebook imposes a false sense of finality, while composing on loose sheets makes the draft too provisional and loosey-goosey. The author determined to write this book on yellow legal pads using black, no, blue ink. White legal pads. It looked for a time as if the author's car might be repossessed before the first draft of this book had been begun in earnest.

The author's best-known story, "The Night of the Chihuaha," has not yet been written down, but he is often asked to tell it at parties. Most listeners agree that it is still getting better with every re-telling, so maybe it's too soon to commit it to a notebook. Or to loose sheets of typewriter paper. Red ink? Pencil?

The author's forthcoming project is a work of non-fiction called *Know Your Rights: How to Fight Repossession and Eviction*. He lives with his mother.

What to Expect

Experiences in the first month vary. You may feel fatigued, nauseous, bloated. Your breasts may feel tender. You may crave certain foods, but food aversions are just as common.

In the second month you may feel dizzy, irritable. You may experience mood swings. By the third month, your appetite will probably increase. Veins thicken in your abdomen and legs.

In the fourth month, any nausea you felt may decrease. Or increase. Or you may feel nauseous for the first time. Your ankles and feet may swell. Experiences vary. You may have trouble concentrating.

By the fifth month, you will likely feel the fetus moving. Leg cramps are not unusual in the sixth or seventh month, and you may have difficulty sleeping. Braxton Hicks contractions begin. You may dream of the baby. You may feel giddy. You may feel like crying. You may cry.

In the ninth month, contractions may wake you.

In the eleventh month, your sleep will almost certainly be disrupted. You may experience mood swings, nipple soreness, pain.

In the thirtieth month, arguing and tantrums are common. You may feel tired, irritable, irrational.

In the 200th month, sleep disruptions often return. You may lie awake waiting for the phone to ring. If you sleep, the phone may wake you. You may imagine that you hear a key in the door. Anxiety is common. You may experience mood swings. You may dream of your baby. Experiences vary.

Cows With Names
Make 3.4 % More Milk

When Brenda was still a teenager she liked to quote those findings to visitors. Most everyone understood that it wasn't really the names that made for better production, but visitors would still chuckle appreciatively when Brenda reeled them off. "That's Mandy Pie with the black circle around her eye, and the one next to her is Foxy for her favorite forage. She'll walk through an acre of alfalfa to get to meadow foxtail. Over by the fence is Honey Lemon. You never know which mood you're going to get from her, the sweet or the sour." Brenda could go on to name any cow within sight. She did her share of work with them every day, after all.

In college she was a dairy science major, even though her father had told her, "Sweet Pie, you'd just be taking over my debts." She had plans for improving the farm. She could supply restaurants with butter and fresh cheeses unlike anything they could get elsewhere. The farm might need a new name.

The first boys Brenda met at school didn't impress her. Like most of the girls in her dorm, she hooked up with guys at parties, but nothing ever came of a night of making out. If she saw those guys again at all, they often didn't remember her name. One morning, Brenda's roommate was happy because the boy she'd had sex with the night before had asked for her phone number. Brenda said, "Do you even hear what you're saying? Right then and there, Brenda was finished with hooking up. She wasn't going to meet the right guy at school.

Her senior year, in the second week of the term, she was waiting in the hallway before Introduction to Finance. "So," said a guy who was waiting next to her, "you're a finance major?" Brenda shook her head, told him she was majoring in dairy science. "Dairy science?" he said. He had blue eyes. Nice eyes, though now his gaze was flitting back and forth between meeting hers and looking anywhere else. She could tell he was struggling to find the next thing to say. He settled on repeating, "Dairy science." Then, "As in cows, huh?" Finally, he held out his hand. "Colin," he said. "Colin Downs. Colin *Tristan* Downs." He smiled.

It wasn't a bad start, but what sealed the deal, over the course of the semester, dinners out, movies, a picnic, and eventually a trip home to meet her parents, were the nicknames that he rained down on her in a succession that promised never to end:

"Ladybug"
"Spark Plug"
"Mama Moo"
"Marmalady"
"Miss Butter"
"Mighty Smacky High Holy Bee-atchy"
"Brenda Pooks"
"Applesauce"

"Sugar Twitch"

"Angel"

Five years later, they were running Summer Peach Creamery together, and although Colin commuted to a job in town and had no hand in managing the herd, he certainly knew Cowzilla from Betty Boop.

Deception Café

At one time, the Fidalgo Island restaurant on highway twenty was called Gisela's Bridgeway Café. If you ordered a cup of coffee, you could be sure it was coffee. But now? You may not taste any hint of chicory. For that matter, the crab meat in the paella may look and taste like real crab. But you have to wonder: Why do they call it the Deception Café?

Listen. The lemon tarts are enchanted. So much as bite into one, and the spell is on. Your small lies will convince. No one will believe you when you tell outrageous truths.

Every other man who enters the Deception Café falls in love with the waitress who glides among the tables. Why is it that a woman so beautiful never smiles? You might wonder if she is hiding her teeth. If you dare to lean very close, you may catch the hint of raw fish on her breath. Where does she live? I followed her from the café one night, all the way down to the beach and to the black water's edge. Before she vanished, she waded in up to her knees. Sea lions barked. She turned her head as if someone had just called her name.

A young man sits very still at one of the outdoor tables. He never orders a thing but only watches the other diners. Why doesn't Kathy, the owner, throw him out? But he is handsome and golden-eyed and sits so very still, almost invisible. He doesn't smile, doesn't show his teeth.

People claim to have seen a mountain lion on the island, but it's a crazy idea. It's not as if a mountain lion could stroll unnoticed across the bridge.

Do you want the truth? The Deception Café takes its name from the channel it overlooks, the cold Pacific waters of Deception Pass. The lemon tarts are very good, but they are only lemon tarts. Trust me.

Egypt

The elder son went before his father and said unto him, "Let me go to the concert next Saturday, for the band is to be Good Charlotte."

And the Old Man said, "Who are you to go to any concert on Saturday when you have been grounded two weeks? And why is the lawn, which ought to have been mowed yesterday, still untouched by any blade?"

And in the morning at breakfast, the father could not drink of his coffee for it tasted of rust, and he complained bitterly to his wife.

And the son said, "Did I not ask you to let me go to the concert? Now the water is turned to rust."

But the father's heart was hard, and he said unto the mother, "Run the cold water a bit to clear the pipes before you make coffee."

And in the evening of the same day, when the father put his feet up to read the paper, there arose a great cry from the living room. "What in God's name?" said the father, and went to see his wife who stood pointing at a frog on the coffee table.

And the younger son was called to make an account of the frog, and he was made to take it back outside and not to bring it again into the house.

And the older son said, "Did I not ask you to let me go to the concert?"

And the next morning, there arose again a great cry, this time from the bathroom where the mother was combing the hair of the younger son. "Lice again?" said the father. "They need to fumigate those kids. I have had it about up to here with that school!"

And the older son said, "It is not the school that keeps me from going to the concert."

But the father's heart was hard, and he gave his son such a look.

And in the evening of the same day, the father said, "Who left the screen door standing open? The house is full of flies!"

And the son said, "Let me go to the concert, for all the guys will be there and I alone of all the guys will not."

And the father said, "You should have thought of that before you went and got yourself grounded."

And upon the morning of the next day, the car would not start, and the father tried to get a ride from a neighbor, but the neighbor's car also was afflicted.

And the father said, "I guess I will have to take the bus."

And the mother said, "Wait a second. What's that on your nose? Honey, you've got a pimple."

And the father said, "I know, I know. At my age."

And the sky darkened, and there was hail, very grievous, such as there was none like it upon the land since last summer.

And the hail smote the windshield of the car that would not start.

And the son said, "Let me go to the concert, else, if you refuse me, I will this afternoon bring locusts into the house."

But the father made no answer, and when he returned at the end of the day, on the kitchen counter he found empty milk jugs, cookie packages, yogurt cups, ice cream cartons, soda cans, and candy wrappers, and all the fruit was gone from the crisper.

And the mother said, "If you wanted to make it a rule that he couldn't have his friends over after school, you should have spelled that out when you grounded him."

And that night, which was to be a night of watching television as a family, a thick darkness befell the room and they saw not one another nor the TV, and the mother said, "Looks like the whole neighborhood is out."

And the son said, "Let me go to the concert, for I am bored out of my skull and have suffered punishment enough."

But the father said, "Pester me no more on this and take heed to thyself; ask not again, for in that hour you ask me again, from that hour will you be grounded until your eighteenth birthday."

And upon the morning of the Saturday, the son had such a headache, like unto death, and he moaned most grievously not for himself, but for the suffering of his parents who must mourn his passing in the knowledge that it had been in their power to grant him a dying wish, yet they had refused.

But the father's heart was harder than the heart of Pharaoh.

And it came to pass that the son listened to the songs of Good Charlotte on his iPod alone in his room, and he did not die.

Donat Bobet Recovers His Wallet

I was having my after-work coffee on a sidewalk in Vieux-Montréal when I heard a familiar voice declaiming from down the street. Only an occasional word or two would rise clearly from the sounds of the city. "...delicate...without a hat...the tower..." Even when I could not make out most of the words, I could hear the rhythms of Donat Bobet reciting one of his poems.

Then there came another voice, shouting, "Get out of here! Scram! Leave my customers alone, you parasite!"

Moments later, here came Donat, wearing a straw hat with a flower in the brim and a white tuxedo jacket with tails. I waved and called him over to my table.

"Ah, hello!" he said. His smile looked half-hearted.

"Have you eaten?" Perhaps hunger would explain why his face seemed so lifeless.

"Thank you," he said, pulling out a chair. "Perhaps just a sandwich." I summoned the waitress, and Donat ordered a sandwich, and also a salad, and also a bowl of soup and a glass of wine and some bread. And a plate of cheese as well.

"But I must repay your generosity," Donat said. He stood up and recited for me, and for any other customers within earshot: "This poem is called 'The North American Fabulism Trading Agreement.'"

The bobbin has a little house.
Send it home.

A word wears another word as a wig.
Pretend not to recognize it.

Geese row south in little boats on a river of maple
leaves and syrup.
It is only polite to stand on the shore, waving goodbye.

We open our arms to the armadillos descending
by parachute.
We will teach them to count to thirty-five in French,
which is more than Texas has ever done.

Why didn't we think of this before?
Now you understand, my darlings, my darlings.
You have been holding the instructions upside down.

He bowed to each of the tables, where other customers ignored him. He sat down with a sigh.

"Are you all right?" I asked him.

"I lost my wallet at the intersection of Saint-Laurent and Sainte-Catherine, where I am always losing my wallet."

"I'm sorry," I said. But what did it mean to always lose

something in the same place? "You mean it was stolen? That's not a good area."

"I lost it. I mean what I say, I am careful with words."

"Did you make a report? Someone might find it and turn it in."

"Someone always does," he said. "I am on my way to the police station."

"To make a report?"

"No. To collect the wallet."

"Someone found it then! Good news!"

"Well..." he said.

I imagined from his expression that the wallet had been recovered, but without its contents. That would depress me, too. When his food came, I let him eat in silence. He finished, and I paid the bill.

"Would you like to come along to the station with me?" His words were more than an invitation. He was as dismayed as I had ever seen him. What he wanted, I thought, was companionship.

"Of course, my friend."

The police station was not very many blocks away, on the rue Sainte-Élisabeth. We went along in silence, except when the poet said, "There are times when I worry about the soul of Montréal." I did not know what to say to that.

We had scarcely entered the police station when a young constable behind the counter said cheerily, "Good evening, M. Bobet."

Donat raised his hand to her in silent greeting.

"Just a minute," she said. "I'll get it from the property desk." She opened a door, disappeared, and then reappeared with a small plastic tray. She turned the tray over, and a leather wallet fell onto the counter along with a plastic bag for what had been inside the wallet: Driver's license, a credit card, some slips of paper. "Do make sure it's all there," said the constable.

Donat sorted through the contents of the bag, putting things back into the wallet. The credit card, I realized, was made of cardboard and said "Moon and Stars Credit." What I had taken for a driver's license was no such thing. "Poetic License," it said, and where there should have been a photo, there was a collage: a man's shoulders and neck topped with a radish and a hat. On the money-sized slips of paper were the texts of poems. He counted these.

"It's all here," he said miserably. "Every bit of it." He signed a form on a clipboard, and we left.

"Donat," I said as we walked, "may I see that wallet?"

He gave it to me. The license bore his name and address. The credit card had an expiration date of *GOODNESS NO*. When Donat wasn't looking, I slipped one of the poems from the wallet into my pocket, then I gave the wallet back to him.

I said, "You're sure it's all there?"

"I checked."

"You're positive?"

He sighed, stopped in his tracks, and made a show of flipping the wallet open. He took out the poems and counted them. He looked at me. He counted a second time, finishing now with a smile. "One of them is missing! Do you know what this means?"

"Yes. That someone in Montréal is a poetry thief."

"It means," Donat said with a smile, "that I must buy you a drink to celebrate!"

Donat buying me a drink. That was a new idea! Around the corner, we found a suitable establishment. I had not yet eaten dinner, but we took a booth and split a bottle of champagne. We toasted the city until I felt dizzy.

"I must go home and have something substantial to eat," I said at last, standing to leave.

"Oh, dear." Donat was patting his pockets. "I know that I offered to pay," he said, "but I seem to have lost my wallet!"

FIVE:
STORY STORIES

The Little Story That Could

Some readers doubted that the story was a story at all. "It's too short. It lacks characters," some said.

"What about a story question?" asked others. "Does this story have a story question? Do the events of this narrative tend to increase tension and thus compel readers to continue? There is nothing at stake in this sequence of events!"

The story was undaunted. True, it was short. It was simple. It wasn't about very much. But a short and simple story might well provide its readers with pleasure. Sometimes a thing is pleasant simply for being unexpected.

"Nothing is unexpected any longer," said another reader. "We've seen it all."

Even so, thought the story, I must do my best.

So the story proceeded from sentence to sentence, line by tidy line, sure of itself. Indeed, as it progressed it felt its confidence grow. Why not? Its words were all spelled correctly. It contained dialogue, which gives any story a bit of drama and the music of imagined voices.

There was some   white space!

There were exclamations for excitement!

¡Aún había una frase en español!

Surely, the story thought, it would find at least one appreciative reader. If one, then why not two? And why not, then, an appreciative editor? Eventually, the story might very well be published, and once published, why shouldn't it win a prize? The story began to positively swagger.

"Don't be so sure," said the story's author, who had some experience with disappointment.

The story made the rounds. It lingered in the offices of editors, one after another.

One after another, the editors said, "Go home. This story is not wanted here."

But why? the story wondered. *Why don't the editors love me?*

The editors did not say.

The story went to the readers who had doubted it. The story said, "What should I do?"

"I like pirate stories," said one reader. "Put in some pirates. And ghosts. And a beautiful girl."

"No," said another reader. "What you need is a philosophical question such as this: 'As solitary, separate, and mortal beings, how can we possibly be redeemed by love?'"

"What you really need," offered a third, "is more figurative language. 'Again and again, the story broke itself upon the adamantine shoals of indifference.'"

"Wait!" cried a fourth reader. "Pirates might be fine. Or philosophy. You might even get away with adamantine shoals—though I doubt it. But don't mix them! Don't put them all in the same story!"

Of course, it was too late. Pirates, philosophy, and adamantine shoals were all already in the story. But the story decided that it would carry on nonetheless, that it would continue to do the best that it could do. It would persist, and its persistence would be its gift. One day, a reader would find the story, read it through all the way to the end, and feel inspired.

The Story You Didn't Read

A woman rows a boat across a mountain lake. Clouds hide the sun now and then. Wind excites the surface of the water, as if many thousands of minnows were striking the surface at once. The woman lets the oars rest, dripping water. She can smell pine and spruce from the shore. A black bird circles overhead, and the woman thinks about the story you didn't read. That story has changed her life. Here in the middle of the lake, she can feel that story rocking her the way the wind rocks the boat.

Two old men drive the highway at night, pulling a rented trailer. The trailer contains all of the worldly goods of one of these men. It's not a big trailer. It's not even full. For miles, they have watched the white lines of the highway without speaking. The man who owns these things sits in the passenger seat, and the other man, the driver, clears his throat and says, "Let me tell you a story." He recounts the events of the story you didn't read. He tells it without the elegance, the precision, that the story has on the page, but he remembers all the important parts. He gets across the beginning, the middle, and the end. When the driver has finished, the men are silent for a while. At last, the driver says, "Well, what did you think of that?" The other man has taken out his handkerchief. He wipes his face. He blows his nose. He puts away the handkerchief. "Thank you," he says. "Thank you for that."

Had you read the story you didn't read, mention of it now would make you feel something that is difficult to express. You would look out the window. You would search your memory for a word that names this feeling, and you would decide that there isn't one, at least not in the English language. You would wonder if, perhaps, there might be a word for it in Japanese.

The Indecisive Story

Once upon a time in a dark, dark wood, there was a story that didn't know what it was. It began with a wolf, but he was no ordinary wolf. No, indeed! He was the wolf king. He had the blackest coat you ever did see, and he spied the world with the yellowest eyes. When the winter winds howled among the wolves and the wolves howled in reply, his voice was the strongest. So it had been for a very long time. If another wolf challenged him, the king fought tooth and claw to remain king. In all the dark, dark wood, there was no wolf to match him.

At the same time, the story observed that the elaborate communication system of wolves usually forestalls wolf-on-wolf aggression in a pack. The other wolves knew that the black-coated male was their alpha, and their body posture demonstrated this awareness whenever he approached. Lower-ranking wolves held their heads down, their ears back, and they curled their lips in a submissive grin. Young males that thought they were up to challenging the alpha might hold their heads a little higher, let the tips of their ears rise slightly, testing. And the alpha's answering snarl would usually be enough to make them revert to a more submissive pose. But not every challenger would back down, and the most common cause of death among wolves is attack by other wolves.

This story about wolves was also a story of men. One man in particular. Luc, he was called. Luc, the king of the gypsies. He carried a revolver in his pocket, a six-shooter that he cleaned each night while he leaned against the side of his wagon. Outside, that is. Out where every member of the gypsy band could see him. He wasn't subtle about the bulge the gun made in his embroidered jacket, either. That was on purpose. The revolver focused attention. If any of the young men, alone or with help, made a play to take over, they'd take his revolver and think that they'd done the job. They wouldn't know about the little two-shot snubby he concealed in his belt until it was pumping lead between their eyes. One of these days, though, the guns wouldn't be enough. Luc knew that. And he knew that day was coming soon. He couldn't knock the spots off a playing card at a hundred paces any longer. The young men, they were beginning to figure this out.

Luc's wife loved him with a passion as wide and deep as the sea. When he told her that he must go, and go alone, she couldn't believe what he was saying. With her brown eyes flecked with gold, she looked deep into his chestnut eyes flecked with an even darker brown. "Didn't you say that we would always be together?" she said. The muscles in his jaw hardened. He would not answer even when she touched his face with her fingertips, grazed the rough stubble that was like armor for the soft skin beneath, a softness that she and she alone truly knew. "It's what I have to do," he said. "I can't stay with the camp. My time here is over. The torch passes to younger men. But where I'm going, it's no place for a woman." He wasn't asking her to understand, she realized. He was asking her to endure, and that was something she knew how to do.

Alone. He lived alone in a little cabin, alone, alone. The winter wind blew in the trees, shaking down the sugar snow. What few visitors he had spoke no human words, but left their sigils scratched upon the whiteness: the triune tracks of jays, or the mousy trail that ended with the fluffy swipe, the erasure made by an owl's wing. And in this loneliness he found himself afoot, unarmed, for what had he to fear, alone, alone? Late one day, shadows in the lee of trees began to stir as he approached. They were wolves, winter-thin in the haunches, with eyes burning gold in the crepuscular light. Low growls in their throats, they closed upon him, and in the next heartbeat they might spring. Suddenly, a roar! A black beast, more massive than the rest, bounded from the circle. But this was no leap for the throat. The black wolf landed beside the man, stood as if a sentinel. It growled with a sound the man could feel in his knees. As one, the pack turned and melted into forest. All save the one, the elder wolf, which turned before it vanished, turned and met the man's gaze with its yellow eyes.

The story was easy. The story was easy to read. The story was about a man. The man lived in the woods. There were some wolves in the woods. The wolves did not attack the man. The man did not know why. Then the man was cutting wood. He was cutting wood for the fire. A wolf came close. The man saw the wolf. He knew the wolf. The wolf had a black coat. The wolf had yellow eyes. It was the wolf from before. It was the wolf that did not attack. The wolf was all alone. The wolf looked old. The wolf looked tired. "Come inside," said the man. "Come inside the house." The wolf came inside the house. The wolf lay down. It lay down beside the fire. Now the man knew. He knew why the wolf did not attack.

A Quiet Story

The story had very little to say.

The Story That Went Over Your Head

In a room overlooking the street, you sat near a reading lamp and concentrated on the pages of a difficult story. The author used words like nematic and cognomen. The names of the story's characters all began with the letter Y. As if that weren't bad enough, the text was sprinkled with unpronounceable words in a foreign tongue: trychtýř and zvláštnost, for example.

While you concentrated on the story, a commotion erupted on the street. A woman—her name was Ynés—was yelling at her boyfriend, Ysmael. Ordinarily, you might have gone to the window to see what was happening, but you didn't even hear them, so intent were you upon deciphering the story.

Ynés held a box of condoms that she had just found in the glove compartment of Ysmael's car. She shook the box at Ysmael. She used words like lying and pig. When she lapsed into another language, the words were ones that you could have said yourself with a little practice: *pendejo* and *libertina*, for example. Had you been paying attention, you could have figured out their meanings from context.

Ysmael held his hands out in front of himself as he offered some sort of explanation. You didn't see this, though. You squinted at the page. You thought to yourself, Agrestically? Is that even a real word?

Ynés, meanwhile, reached into the glove compartment a second time. She brought out a pistol. Other people on the street started shouting. She fired without aiming.

In the middle of a sentence—*crack!*—the bullet pierced your window and tore a hole in your ceiling. You looked up. You thought, *What the hell was that?*

The Story You Might Have Read Instead of This Story

It wants the best for you, the story you might have read instead of this one. It really does. Even though you have found yourself on this page, even though the story you might have read feels a bit abandoned on another page far away, it understands. You can't read everything. There's only so much time for fiction. Other things need doing, and even if other things didn't need doing, your reading time would nonetheless be limited. You're going to die, after all.

(It's the business of literature to remind you of this, and even the story you might have read would want you to remember: *Gentle reader, you are going to die.* The story you might have read would have reminded you in a more roundabout fashion.)

The story you might have read is sorry that it missed its chance to transport you. That's what it would have done. Rather than referring to itself and reminding you that you are interpreting black marks on a page, the story you might have read would have carried you imaginatively to some other setting. A Jamaican beach, say, where a man plays a steel drum. Or the airless plains of the moon. Or a schoolyard on a Sunday afternoon when no children are about and a young woman on her hands and knees looks for something in the grass. But not every story aspires to transport you. Some stories, like the one you chose to read, only remind you that you are right where you are at the moment, that the steel drum and the moon and the lost object in the grass are all merely words.

(You're not somewhere else, gentle reader. You are right here, reading words on a page.)

Here you are, then, reading a story about the experience of reading a story, while the story you might have read wishes you well. The story you might have read hopes that you will not spend all your time reading. It hopes you will get some fresh air. It hopes that when you are out getting some air, you will happen to see a young woman on her hands and knees looking for something in the schoolyard grass, and you will say to her, "What are you looking for? Can I help?" and she will look up at you, and you will be struck by the color of her eyes, the depth of her gaze, her beauty; you will hold your breath, and you will think to yourself in an eternal moment, *I am going to die.*

Meanwhile, someone else is reading the story that you might have read. That reader might have instead read this story—the story you are reading now—but now never will. And this story wants the best for that reader. It really does.

A Likely Story

One day, the writer threw up his hands. "I've had it," he said to his wife. She was his second wife, actually. He had divorced the first one in graduate school. "I've been doing this for years, writing these damn stories. And for what? So that I can walk into a bookstore and see all the books that aren't my book? So that I can plead with people, 'Please, read this! You'll be glad you did!' Who reads the magazines, except for other writers who hope to publish in them?"

"Lie down," said his wife. "Do you want a cool cloth for your forehead?"

"I mean it this time!" insisted the writer. "What stories are left to tell, anyway? They've all been told. Everything's been said. Does the world need another story about a young writer whose marriage falls apart when he goes to graduate school? Do we need any stories about pirates, or pretty young girls, or the making of stories? I'm sick of hard work, day after day, in the face of utter indifference!"

"Shh," said his wife, as if she were soothing a puppy in a thunderstorm.

"I'm finished!" the writer said. He tore open his chest, and he pulled out the story stuff, all the red threads of it. "Out!" he said. He threw the story stuff into the trash can. He carried it to the curb.

But the garbage men wouldn't take it. It was still there after they had come and gone.

"No more!" the writer said. He dumped the story stuff into the compost heap. But it didn't rot. Day after day, it was the same sticky redness.

"All right then," said the writer. "It will burn!" He gathered leaves and wood and old manuscripts, fuel for a funeral pyre. He dumped the story stuff on top.

"Are you sure about this?" said his wife.

"Never more sure!" The writer set the pile ablaze. The red mass on top only smoked at first, but then, as the fire burned hotter, it popped and sizzled and smoked. At last it burst into flame. The smoke blackened.

"Aha!" said the writer. He danced. "Aha ha ha ha ha!"

The smoke didn't rise very far. It sort of hovered in the yard. But the writer didn't care. He was free. Free! He danced around the dying flames.

"What about this smoke?" asked the wife, waving her hand before her face.

The writer shrugged. It would clear out by morning, he supposed. He suggested that they go inside.

However, the smoke was heavier inside the house than it had been in the yard.

"You should have closed the windows," said his wife.

"It will clear," he told her. And it already was clearing, in a way. The smoke was concentrating, condensing, congealing here and there. Black spots formed on the walls. This spot had an opening in the middle, like the letter *o*. That one looked like an *e*. The writer rubbed one of the letters with his finger. It fell to the floor. "It's all right," he said. "They come off."

"But what about later?" said his wife. "What if they set, like stains?"

There were letters condensing on the furniture, on white shirts in the closet. The writer and his wife went around the house, brushing letters onto the floor wherever they were forming. The writer took off his shirt and used it to smack letters from the ceiling. Finally, the smoke thinned to a barely detectable haze. Finally, there were no more letters forming, nothing to wipe off. The writer and his wife fell into their bed, exhausted.

In the morning, when the writer got out of bed to go to the bathroom, his wife said, "What's that?"

"What's what?"

"On your back," she said.

The writer stood in front of the mirror and looked over his shoulder. There were rows and rows of tiny black letters. He rubbed at them. They were indelible, like a fine, spidery tattoo.

They formed a story.

SIX

A Fine and Private Place

Susan starts to see dullness in the eyes of other people before she feels it herself. In late September, the neighbor walking his dog doesn't lift his gaze from the pavement to greet her. By October, the woman behind the counter at the underground station—the one who had a smile for everyone in July—looks right through Susan. Susan feels it herself not long after that. The shadows, even in the middle of a sunny day, have turned blue and cold. Day by day, she sleeps later and later.

Articles in the newspaper advise tests for vitamin D. Her husband, coming home to find the baby wet and crying, dishes still piled in the sink, and no sign of dinner, thinks that Susan should see the doctor about a pill. Maybe there's a new one this year, a better one. The next morning, he tries to get her up early, to get both her and the baby dressed for a turn in the park. "I can't," she says, and when he insists he succeeds only in making her cry, even though she knows he's trying to help. After he is gone, she does manage to go to the park with the baby. The sun rides low in the sky. Brown leaves blanket the ground beneath the trees.

She doesn't want vitamin D or a new pill. Sometimes the old ways are the best. At home, she and the baby nap together, and then Susan calls the sitter.

In the park again, under a tree, Susan lies down on the ground. She smells the earth underneath the fallen leaves and cold grass. She sleeps a little, then wakes up with, for the first time in days, the definite will to do something. With her bare hands, she sweeps away leaves, tears through the turf, and clutches the black soil. She digs, handful after handful, down and down into the earth. When the hole is deep, very deep, she stands in it and pulls leaves in behind her. She lies down at the bottom. She hugs her knees. She remembers a line from some poem or song: The grave's a fine and private place. And it is. She sleeps, at last, as much as she wants to sleep.

Susan is one of the last to wake. Groundskeepers are filling in other holes, planting flower beds in the earth turned for them months ago by sleepers. The walk home is a long one. Dirt clings to her hair. Her clothes are alive with tiny companions. Some of them drop from clay-stiffened seams as she walks, and they crawl away between the paving stones, back toward darkness and safety. Susan knows she looks a fright. She really needs to brush the loamy taste from her teeth. And at home, what will she find? The sitter is a pretty girl, and her husband, well, a man's a man. She thinks these thoughts, but doesn't worry. She'll handle it. She can handle anything. Susan smiles at everyone she meets, whether they smile back, look away, or stare. At this time of year, with the trees budding out, with daffodils springing up everywhere, she's a goddess whether she looks the part or not.

Aerodynamics for Girls

It was still dark out when Reetha crept down the stairs. Her father was already at the table, dipping the corner of his toast into a runny egg yolk. Just above a whisper, Reetha said, "Good morning, Daddy."

He nodded.

Reetha took an apple out of the refrigerator, rinsed it, and then cut out a wedge of about one sixth. She considered the wedge, then cut it in half lengthwise and put one of the wedges back into the apple as if she were replacing a puzzle piece. She wrapped the apple in plastic and put it in the refrigerator. She washed the knife. When she turned around, her father was watching her. He looked like he might say something. He didn't. Instead, he wiped his mouth and put his plate on the table edge to catch the crumbs he swept up with his hand. Reetha ate her apple slice one nibble at a time, watching her father take his plate to the sink, wash it, dry it, and put it away. He threw out the paper napkin. Then he washed the frying pan, dried it, and put it away. He upended the toaster over the sink to shake out any crumbs that might have fallen while the bread was toasting. Then he cleaned the sink, wiped it down with the dish towel, and went to put the towel in the washing machine.

They left the house together as the sun was rising. Night

insects had stopped stirring, and in the morning chill the day insects weren't very active yet. Getting out of the house required no special attention to the screen doors. That was one of the advantages of starting the day so early.

Her father didn't offer to drop her off on the way to Brookhaven Hardware. Probably it had never occurred to him. Anyway, she needed the exercise she got from walking. At school, she had to wait a little for Mrs. Pinnock to arrive and let her into the building. Only one time had Mrs. Pinnock asked Reetha why she came to school so early every day. Because she had never asked again, she was one of Reetha's favorite teachers. Reetha would stay in Mrs. Pinnock's social studies room and do homework until eight, when the library opened. In the library, she could read *Essence* or *YM* until it was time for her to go to home room.

For lunch, she ordered the soup and took her time spooning up the broth. From the solid food at the bottom of the bowl, she chose two pieces of chicken, one noodle, one carrot piece, and all the celery. Celery was okay. She stayed after classes for French Club, but she skipped the last part of the meeting where they were talking about the bake sale and Missy Dexter would not shut up about cream pastries and seven layer tortes. Reetha took the long way home.

Outside the porch door, a yellow jacket buzzed around. Reetha watched it fly, trying to make out its wings, but in motion they were invisible. She took her book bag from her shoulder and held it at her side, so she could move fast. While she waited for the yellow jacket to go away she noticed a couple of flies on the screen door, so she shooed them off. They settled on the door again, which would be okay, she decided, as long as they stayed on the door, on the outside.

The yellow jacket flew away. Reetha opened the screen
door, slipped inside the porch. The door slapped shut against
the frame. She looked at the screen. The flies were gone. The
motion had set them to buzzing around. Reetha listened,
making sure they were still on the other side of the screen.
The only thing she heard was something that could have
been the growl of distant thunder. She turned around and
scanned for any sign of flies on the porch. She looked from
the pest strips in the corners to the pieces of flypaper tacked
around the door. The flypaper was spotless. Mama always
threw out any pieces that had flies stuck on them, or that she
thought had lost some of their stickiness over time. It was a
good thing Reetha's father could buy the flypaper and pest
strips at wholesale.

Reetha waited a little longer to be sure, then opened
the second screen door and went into the house. From the
kitchen, her mother's voice: "Girl, why you home from school
so late?"

"French club, Mama. Every Wednesday. I told you."

Her mother appeared holding a flyswatter, the bleach
bottle, and a rag. "You ain't let any in, I hope!"

"I was careful."

"You make sure." Her mother handed her the flyswatter,
bleach, and rag. "You stay put til you made sure."

"Mama, I'm sure." She tried to hand the things back.

"Well then how do they get in? I got one today, and it
wasn't me who let it in. You stand right there. You stand a
vigil on them."

Her mother went back into the kitchen. Reetha stood

still for a moment or two longer, then crept into the dining room, hung the flyswatter on its hook, and put the bleach bottle underneath the end table. She hadn't used the rag, but now it had been handled enough that it would need to be washed. She took it to the washing machine and added it to the rags soaking in bleach. Then she snuck upstairs with her book bag to do her physics homework. The lesson was on electrical potential, which Reetha understood well enough even though it was boring. She went back and reread the early chapter on vectors again, especially the examples that had to do with aerodynamics. Later, she heard the sounds of the car in the driveway, her father's footsteps, her mother's voice asking him about flies. His silence.

Still later, her bedroom door opened without warning. She wasn't allowed to have a lock. Her mother squinted at her, seemed satisfied about something. "All right," she said. "You come set the table, then."

At dinner, Reetha removed the stainless steel plate cover from her clean, empty plate, took the glass lid from the first serving dish, and served herself nine kernels of white corn. She put the cover back on the serving dish before passing it to her father.

"That all the corn you going to have?" her father said. "Hardly a bite?"

"I'm not very hungry, Daddy." She served herself some mustard greens, avoiding all but two of the ham cubes.

"A girl can be too skinny. For boys."

"Oh, no," her mother said. "That's the last thing we need, some boy." She said it as if the word *boy* named a variety of fly. Reetha imagined herself trying to bring a boy, say that

Carlton Williams boy, into the house through the front porch. The flypaper would reach out and grab him. Reetha could try to pull him free, but he'd be stuck there until Mama came to throw him out. Reetha covered her mouth with her hand.

"Oh," said her mother. "You think boys are something funny now?"

"No, Mama." Reetha passed the greens to her father.

After dinner, Reetha's mother scolded her for leaving leftover food uncovered and unattended in the kitchen. "That breeds them!"

"Mama, there has to be a fly in the house already to lay eggs." Reetha scraped the leftovers into the kitchen garbage, then tied the garbage bag shut. "They don't just rise up out of spoiled food."

"I know that! Don't get lippy with me!" Outside the house, trees swayed in a sudden wind. Thunder rolled somewhere west of town. "I know all about flies laying eggs. That ain't the only thing I know! I know how a girl gets a baby! What do you know about that?"

"Mama, not this again. I'm tired. I've got my homework to finish, and then I'm going to bed."

"I'll look in on you."

"I know you will, Mama." Reetha kissed her mother's forehead. "Good night."

"You are about the earliest to bed I ever knew."

Reetha said nothing to that. She went up to her room. She turned out her bedroom light and watched the storm build in the growing darkness. Trees bent lower and lower in the wind.

She removed the screen from her window and climbed out onto the roof. She put the screen back in place. If her mother came into her bedroom, it would be hard enough to explain what she was doing on the roof without also having to answer for the missing screen.

It wasn't raining yet, but it smelled like rain. Reetha went to the crown of the roof. She felt light, even a little dizzy.

Lightning flashed. Reetha faced into the wind. She held her arms out at her sides, palms down. She cupped her hands very slightly, so the wind rushing by would have to go farther over the top of her hands than it did underneath her palms. At first she wasn't sure she felt anything.

Again, lightning flashed, and this time the boom of thunder shook her bones. The first fat drops of rain fell cold and stinging against her skin. She kept her arms out, kept her hands in the shape illustrated in her physics book, the cross-section of a wing. At first she wasn't sure, but now she thought she could feel it. Not nearly enough, but detectable: gentle pressure beneath her hands. Lift.

War Gods

1.Problem Child

At the first clatter of spears, Ares would race from Olympus to join in. He didn't care who won, but killed warriors on either side, evening the odds to keep the game alive.

Wounded, he always came to his father. Zeus bound up the injuries of this perverted god, his child, the cursed fruit of his union with Hera. Is it any wonder that their marriage bed was cold?

2. The Case for War

To kneeling priests, the taloned god spelled out his terms:

A great sun temple.

Constant flower wars for captives.

One warrior sacrificed for every temple step.

War for planting. War for harvest. War everlasting, in Huitzilopochtli's name. "Do this, and I will protect you."

"Protect us from what, Great Lord?"

"From those gods who are even worse than I am."

The priests trembled to think of it, and obeyed.

3. Theogeny

Skanda, god of war, slew the demon Taraka, the Invincible. There was peace at last.

"Ha! Did you see him wielding six weapons?" said Agni, god of fire. "That's my boy!"

"I saw him fight brilliantly," answered Shiva, "if you mean my son, Skanda."

"*My* son, Skanda," said Agni.

"Skanda, *my child*," insisted the Destroyer, picking up his trident.

Agni readied his fire dart. The other gods chose sides.

Donat Bobet's Tattoo

What do I know about consoling the bereaved? I know from my own experiences that one loss is not like another, that grief finds its own way. And yet I wanted to do something for Jason Langford. I thought that the thing to do was introduce him to Donat Bobet, though I could not have said why this seemed like a possible antidote for Langford's sorrow. Lanford was my junior colleague. I did not know him well enough to call him my friend, and was unlikely to. He was quite a bit younger than me. I admired him. I admired him for the pain that he had taken on.

I met Langford at his apartment. He looked as if he had just awakened from a nap, but he had looked that way at work recently, all day and everyday. We rode the Metro toward Vieux-Montreal, and for the entire journey, he spoke only when I asked him a question. He stared at nothing. I began to feel that he was the one doing me a favor, and not the other way around. We were not close to begin with. Perhaps I should have left him alone, instead of badgering him to join me for dinner in the home of my poet friend.

Bobet's apartment building is not much to look at, but Langford seemed to come out of his trance a little when he saw the words scrawled in black marker on the peeling paint of the apartment door: "Magnificent ornately carved doors of and oriental motif." We knocked. The poet admitted us. After introductions, I spoke to Bobet about the dinner he was preparing for us—green beans and ground turkey in ginger soy sauce. Langford went around the room, inspecting the writing on the walls, the rectangles that declared themselves to be famous paintings or, in one case, an antique map of the Orient. As he spoke to me, Bobet watched Langford.

"Tell about yourself," Bobet prompted when we had come to table.

"There is little to tell," said my colleague.

Bobet looked at me, then at Langford. "You work together, the two of you?"

"Yes."

Langford was not going to volunteer anything, so it was up to me. I told Donat Bobet about Langford's girlfriend, and how she had taken ill with a disorder that slowly drained the life from her, year by year. There was no promise between them when she began to have symptoms. He might well have left her and gotten on with life, and no one would have blamed him. She had her family—two sisters and a brother, and her parents. With her, Langford could look forward to no future but the painful one of watching her die. Yet he had remained faithful, had visited her in her sick bed at her parents' home, then in the hospital, and later in the invalid home. At the end, he was at her bedside. I considered that an impressive sacrifice by a young man. When I had finished telling all of this to Bobet, I said to Langford, "She was lucky to have you."

"I was lucky to know her," Langford said.

Bobet said, "And now you are desolate, because you imagine that she is dead."

"I imagine nothing," Langford told him. " I saw her die. I was holding her hand."

"My friend," said Bobet, "I saw you admiring my paintings before dinner. Who would imagine that a poet of my background could have such treasures hanging on his walls? I grew up on a farm, poor, miserable. And now I live in this apartment, with this magnificent view—" He gestured at the window that overlooked the alley. On the window glass were written the words, *view of the Saint-Laurent.* "—in the most beautiful city in North America. Now, do you think a man makes such a transition, from pigs in the countryside to the height of luxury in the heart of old Montréal, by giving up? By surrendering?" He touched Langford's sleeve. "Trust me. She is alive."

Langford gave him a weak smile. "I appreciate what you're trying to do..."

"Do you? Do you really?"

"She's gone," Langford said. There were tears in his eyes.

"You are no hero," Bobet said, returning to his dinner.

"That is cold, what you just said," I scolded.

"No, I mean it," said Bobet. Eyes on his food, he gestured at Langford with his fork. "I am glad it was Orpheus who undertook an errand into the underworld, and not this young man."

Langford stared down at his plate. I regretted having brought him. I steered the conversation to politics, to the food. The moment receded. Langford and I did not stay long after the dishes were cleared.

I retained a hope that the evening at Bobet's

apartment—uncomfortable though that one moment was—might have been good for Jason Langford in some way. But he never spoke to me at work about our visit to the poet, and day after day, week after week, he continued to live under the shadow of death. In time, I knew, that shadow would lighten of its own accord. In time, he would join the rest of us.

Meanwhile, I went on visiting Bobet as before, dining with him now and then giving him a little money to support his art. Usually, we ate in his apartment, though occasionally I took him to a restaurant. It was on one of the latter occasions, in a well-lit Chinese restaurant up by the Olympic Park, that I noticed the pink marks on his forehead. "What's that?" I said.

"What?"

"Here." I touched my own forehead in the corresponding place.

"Ah," he said. "It's meant to be subtle." He moved his hair aside, faced me, and leaned closer. I leaned, too. It was a tattoo in ink so faint as to be barely visible. Letters. Words. I squinted to read as he said, "I've had it for weeks, since we had dinner with that young man."

The words were written backwards, I realized. You'd be able to read them in a mirror. They said, *She lives.*

"Oh," I said. "I wonder what Langford will think when he sees that!"

"Do you imagine," Bobet said, "that I did it for him?"

Tourist Photography

"Good day!" said Donat Bobet when I opened my door to him. "A very good day indeed! Are you ready?"

"Ready for what?" I said. My only ambitions for the day were to wash my clothes, pay some bills, and perhaps take a stroll in the park to enjoy my Saturday.

"We live in a destination city," said Donat, "a city that people come to see. The weather is very fine. I have the necessary equipment..." I did not immediately know what the brown plastic cube in Donat's hands might be. It had a round little red window in the center of one side, and a fraying black strap. Only when he turned the cube did I see the tan knob, tan button, and the unmistakable lens. In English below the lens were the words *Brownie Holiday Camera*. "We are off to make some tourist photographs! Come! Come!"

Donat took me by the elbow and drew me out of my apartment. "Hold on a minute," I started to say, but he had already closed my door behind us. "Tourist photographs?"

"What shall it be?" said the poet. "The clock tower in the old port? Olympic Stadium? Notre Dame?" As we stepped outside, I wondered if I should go back for a sweater.

But summer was almost upon us, and under this clear sky the city would grow warmer by the hour. "What do you think?" Donat continued. "The Biodome? The Botanical Gardens? Have you no opinion?"

"We aren't tourists," I told him. "We live here. I have seen those places already!"

"Seen them, yes. Is that all that photography is to you? Seeing?" said Donat. "Aha! The Oratoire Saint-Joseph du Mont-Royal, yes?"

As we rode the Metro to Côte-de-Neiges, I looked at the camera. It must have been fifty years old. "I'm surprised you can still get film for that," I said.

Donat shrugged. "I like the shape," he said. "I like how it feels in my hands."

The walk from the station was uphill all the way, and I was glad to be out in the sun rather than cooped up with my laundry. As we approached the basilica from below, I stopped for a moment to consider the white stone walls and columns, the great arched window, the dome of green copper. "This would make a nice picture," I said, but Donat kept walking. Only when we were at the bottom of the steps did he begin to look through his view finder.

"Ah, this is irresistible," he said at last, but still did not press the shutter. Instead, he went up the steps, placing himself in the setting that he had just approved. "Now we wait," he said.

"For what?"

"For the tourists, naturally!"

We did not have to wait long. A coach pulled into the parking lot, disgorging passengers who clustered together waiting for a few words from their guide. Then some of them walked up the steps, past where Donat and I sat, on into the sanctuary. Others drifted this way and that in the parking lot, lifting cameras now and then, trying for the right angle, the most dramatic perspective. One by one, they came to the bottom of the steps and discovered the shot that Donat had discovered before. When they raised their cameras, Donat raised his. They pressed their shutter buttons. Donat's camera went click at the same time.

What the tourists made of this, I can't say. No one got angry, asked what Donat was up to, or seemed especially bothered. Some of them stopped after they had walked past us on the steps to look back from a distance. A few conferred. I imagine they were saying, "What's that fellow up to?" But none of them spoke to us.

"I think that's enough," said Donat, standing. As we rode the metro back to his neighborhood, he told me, "When one looks at a city, it is well to remember that the city gazes back." Later, in his apartment, Donat opened an old-fashioned photo album and said, "Now to add the new images!"

"But don't you first have to..." I started to say. Donat looked at me with a little smile that said, Film? A superfluous extravagance!

The black pages of the photo album bore white paper photo corners as if each page had once held six or eight images. Now, though, all that remained were the corners and, in silver ink, Donat's writing. *Tourist photo, rue de la Gauchetière. Tourist photo, Carré Phillips. Tourist photo, The Illuminated Crowd.* Donat turned to a page that sported corners but no writing. Three times he wrote: *Tourist photo, Oratoire Saint-Joseph.*

"There," he said, examining his work.

"Three?" I said. "You took more than that."

"Oh, yes, I know," he told me. "But photography is the art of selection." Looking at the black page, he frowned. "Selection, yes, and arrangement. I try to compose with care, yet look at what I've done!"

I looked, but I could see nothing wrong with what he had written. The silver letters were neat and well-ordered. Everything was spelled as it should be. I said so.

"In every image of these tourists, I have aimed the camera too low." He closed the album with a sigh. "Alas. I've cut off all their heads!"

Good Neighbors

The Really Horrible Neighbors Upstairs had made life miserable for Sanjay and Jamila. The mother in her cloud of tobacco, the father who never answered a smile with a smile, the dirty children—they all apparently wore boots and never took them off. Ever. *Clomp-clomp-clomp-clomp!* The children getting up in the night for a drink of water made it sound as if there were a pony upstairs. What is more, Sanjay and Jamila really needed their parking space. Jamila worked a late shift, putting Sanjay through school. By the time she came home the town was dark and silent. Their parking space was well-lit and close to the building, but the neighbors upstairs had always parked in the reserved spot. Jamila would have to park in one of the unmarked spaces in the dark corner of the lot. There was no reasoning with the neighbors. Jamila spoke to them politely. Sanjay talked to them a little less politely, but was nonetheless civil. Still, *clomp clomp clomp* at all hours. Still, the neighbors' car in the reserved space. Even when Sanjay took it up with the manager, who wrote a letter, the neighbors still parked where they pleased. Worse, Sanjay suspected them of throwing birdseed from their balcony into his little flower garden. How else to explain the tiny yellow seeds, the constantly sprouting weeds?

When Sanjay completed his degree, they resolved that in their next apartment they would be on the uppermost floor.

But they would not be the Horrible Neighbors to someone else, just because they were on top. They would take their shoes off inside the house, naturally, as any civilized person does. But even in their stocking feet or slippers, they would tread the wooden floors gently.

And so it was. In their new apartment, they lived on the third floor. They did not play loud music. They did not even own a television.

One day, when Sanjay was at work there was a knock at the door. Jamila answered to find an elderly woman in the hallway. Jamila had seen her before in the foyer, where the mailboxes were. "My dear," said the woman, "I'm terribly sorry, but could you ask your husband not to put his shoes on until he has come all the way down the stairs? He makes such a racket in the morning."

"Oh, dear," said Jamila. "We had no idea. Of course I will speak to him. I'm Jamila, by the way. Would you like to come in for tea?"

"You must speak up," said the woman, holding a hand to her ear.

"Would you like a cup of tea?"

"Tea?" said the old woman, making sure. "Thank you, yes. Thank you, that's very kind."

The old woman's name was Varek. Jamila could not guess how old she might be. She had the translucent skin of someone very old indeed, and she asked Jamila to repeat herself so often that Jamila marveled that Sanjay's footsteps could be disturbing her in the least. Nevertheless, Jamila took up the matter with her husband that night.

"Of course, it's no trouble to carry my shoes down the stairs," he said. "Which apartment does she live in?"

Jamila told him. He thought it was curious that his footsteps on the stairs should bother her. She wasn't that close to the stairwell.

The next time Mrs. Varek complained, it was about the creaking floor.

"But," said Jamila, again pouring tea like a good neighbor, "there is an entire floor between us. Are you sure it's not the neighbors directly above you?"

"The people in that apartment are quiet as mice," said Mrs. Varek. "I'm terribly sorry, but you know how these floors squeak. If you could only be careful not to step too often in the places that make noise."

Later, Sanjay said, "Well, it's a little strange. She's hard of hearing, you say? Yet the squeaking floor two flights above troubles her? Still, it's not much trouble to take care where we step."

For several weeks after that, Jamila did not happen to see Mrs. Varek at the mailboxes. She was surprised, then, to answer her door and find Mrs. Varek leaning against a walker. "I am not well," the old woman said. When she took one hand from the walker, her whole arm shook. "I'm terribly sorry. Terribly sorry. But I need my rest. The sound of your voices keeps me up!"

She declined tea this time.

Home from work, Sanjay said, "How can our voices carry that far!"

"Shh," said Jamila. "Perhaps through the water pipes."

"It's absurd!" Sanjay said.

"Please, lower your voice," Jamila pleaded. "Let's not be like those people who lived above us."

Softly, Sanjay said, "We are nothing like those people."

"You used to speak to me mostly in whispers," breathed Jamila.

"I remember," Sanjay whispered. He smiled.

They woke one night to the flashing lights of the ambulance. Mrs. Varek had suffered a stroke. Even though they had seen the paramedics take her away on a stretcher, Jamila and Sanjay still walked gingerly and whispered for a time. Then, at the mailboxes, Jamila heard from another neighbor that the old woman was dead.

"Well," said Sanjay in a voice that now seemed loud, "we were good neighbors to the end."

"Were we?"

"We were accommodating! You had her in for tea! Why are you wearing such a face? You look guilty!"

"It's sad," she said. "We should have asked her to dinner."

"And if we had, would she have lived forever?"

They did not speak of the old woman after that. But one night, very deep in the night, when a ringing telephone is almost always a mistake or terrible news, the telephone rang. Sanjay picked it up. He cleared his throat. "Hello?" he said. "Hello?"

The phone line hissed and crackled.

"Hello," he said. Then, "Hello!"

Faintly, barely audible under the static of solar wind and the crackle of stars came a voice he didn't recognize, saying his wife's name.

"It's a bad connection," he said handing the phone to her. He got back in bed.

"Yes?" Jamila said into the phone. "Hello? Yes? Hello? Are you there?"

"Your husband," said a familiar voice that Jamila could not place at first. "I'm terribly sorry. Your husband is snoring."

Hello, Gorgeous!

Long ago, in his twenties, he had been something of a Romeo. He met girls at his job in the shoe department. After kneeling in front of them and squeezing to feel the bones of their feet through the thin leather, it was no trouble at all to ask for their phone numbers at the cash register. He went to church every Sunday and met girls there. Even better, he could stroll across the college campus looking for pretty faces. Some girls showed him their engagement rings, said they had a steady guy, or just told him to get lost. He didn't mind. Sometimes he even struck up a conversation after he had already spotted the diamond ring. He just liked talking to girls.

He did more than talk, but not a lot more. Those were innocent times. A date consisted of meeting at a soda fountain or maybe riding the bus together to see a movie at the Oriental. A walk to her door. Chaste kisses. An early goodnight. College girls had dorm curfews. Working girls had parents or, at the very least, roommates who expected them home by ten.

He didn't mind. He thought about sex as much as any young man, but he thought of himself as a gentleman who would be ashamed to get a girl in trouble. Besides, his biggest thrill was meeting someone new. Three or four times a day, at least, he would see a girl who he just couldn't stop looking at. *Hello, gorgeous!* he would think. If he said to her, "Heaven called. They're missing an angel," he meant it. If he had two dates in the same day—one in the afternoon and another after he had left the first girl at her door—it wasn't because he was inconstant. He was, in fact, constantly enchanted.

His life changed when he had saved enough to buy a car, a used Bel Aire. He could take girls to drive-in movies or park by Sloan's Lake to watch the stars. One thing started leading to another. In a year, he was married and had a son. A year after that, he was selling real estate instead of shoes.

He wasn't unhappy. But he didn't stop noticing other women. His wife said it shamed her, the way he stared. So he did his best to change. If he caught himself admiring a woman other than his wife, he would deliberately turn away and say the Lord's Prayer under his breath. By the time he was thirty, he had cured himself.

Through the decades that followed, he was steady. He worked hard and was a good provider. He bought a house. Later, a bigger house. The cars in the driveway were always new. He didn't think he was unhappy. He didn't think about happiness at all. He had responsibilities.

At some point, he broke his own rule and started meeting clients on Sundays. There was college to save for. His wife could take the kids to church. Before he was fifty-five, he had both sons and his daughter through university. That same year, cancer took his wife. It was that sudden.

The house was silent as only an empty house can be. Coming home from the office, he would turn on the television even before he had his coat off, just to fill the space with voices. He'd make himself dinner in the microwave, then watch medical shows. Every day he went to the office, but month by month he brought in fewer clients. His younger associates asked him about his plans for retirement.

"Dad," said his eldest on the telephone, "it's been three years. You should get out. You should meet someone."

"By someone, you mean a woman."

"You should travel, anyway. You have years ahead of you. See some sights! What good does it do you to sit around moping?"

He went to Greece because the travel agent said it was a bargain. On the flight over, he read magazine articles about the first signs of stroke and the best vegetables for beating cancer. He looked at his Greek phrase book. He practiced saying "*Thélo éna yatró*" in case he needed medical attention.

The hotel was an all-inclusive resort full of Dutch and French tourists. He ate breakfast, lunch, and dinner in the dining room, alone, listening to the conversations in languages he didn't know. In his street clothes, he walked around the pool once or twice. Women of all ages sunbathed topless, but it made no impression on him. He walked down to the beach and sat under and umbrella for a while, watching the ferries move along the horizon. By breakfast on the third day, he was already tired of what the resort served.

He rented a car and drove away from the water, through olive groves and alongside plots of artichokes. Finally he came to a village where he parked the car and walked. He didn't know he was looking for anything until he found the church. He stood in the doorway. While his eyes adjusted to the dimmer light, he felt awkward, wondering if he should cross himself. Near the door, two old women sat with a box of tapers, speaking in low voices. He put some coins in the platter and they gave him a candle.

It wasn't a big church, but it was crowded with icons. They had been painted directly onto the plaster. From everywhere on the concave ceiling, the arches, the walls, Christ and perhaps a hundred saints returned his gaze. They were serene, comforting, beautiful. So beautiful. He couldn't remember the last time that he'd felt this sensation of awe in the face of beauty.

He lit his candle and for a while stood watching it burn. He said goodbye in English to the women by the door, and they answered him in Greek. He drove out of the village and across the island, putting more distance between himself and the resort. When he came in sight of the sea again, it was along a rocky stretch of coast where the only buildings were hardly more than shacks.

His son had been right to tell him to take a trip. He felt as if he had been asleep a long, long time.

After several kilometers of empty road, he came upon a bright yellow building with a weathered sign that still said, barely, *Taverna*. He hadn't remembered to bring the phrase book. He sat at a table outside in the shade. The girl who brought him a menu couldn't understand his questions, and the menu, all in Greek, didn't help. With gestures, she got him to stand up and follow her into the little kitchen. There he met a middle-aged woman who might have been the girl's mother. They talked about him, he guessed, since they looked at him as they spoke. Then the mother raised her voice. A man's voice answered, then a white-haired fellow appeared with a tray of fish, dripping ice. They all three gestured for him to choose one.

With the fish and fresh lemons, he had a bottle of Coca-Cola because he knew how to ask for it. He ate the fish slowly, both because he wanted to savor it and because it had bones. A car stopped, and a crowd of young female tourists got out jabbering away in some language that wasn't Greek. Russians, maybe. Or Poles.

One of the women happened to turn from her companions and looked his way. He stopped chewing. *Wow!* he thought. She turned back toward her companions, but he couldn't take his eyes from her. Such delicate features! He wondered what her hair smelled like. Then the girl who had served him appeared with menus, and she, too, was beautiful. How had he missed noticing her? Her features were not like the Slavic girl's at all. She was darker, the lines of her face more dramatic. She had more character, but she was no less beautiful. Stunning.

He had forgotten what it was like, to really see young women, to drink in beauty.

Every one of the Slavic women was dazzling. He looked from one to the next, amazed and full of longing. He wanted to take each one into his arms and hold her.

It seemed they spoke no Greek, and the girl with the menus was having no success in getting them to follow her back into the kitchen. So she disappeared.

He did his best to be polite, to look away any time any of the women looked in his direction. But he couldn't help himself. He stared.

The middle-aged mother came out. She was beautiful, too! He wanted to kiss the wrinkles around her eyes. Behind her came the white-haired man, bearing the tray of fish, and...

Oh. My. The old fisherman was stunning. What would it be like to touch the sunburned skin of the old man's face? A golden light surrounded the old man, surrounded all of them, all the young women, and the mother, too. They were all so beautiful. He wanted to gather them all in his arms. Everyone.

He blinked. He wiped his eyes with a napkin. He was filled with joy. And fear. He tried to think back to the article he had read, the first signs of a stroke. And if he was having a stroke, what was that phrase in Greek that meant *I want a doctor*? He couldn't remember it. Every time he tried to recall it, all he seemed to be able to think of was a phrase in English. *Hello, gorgeous!*

SEVEN

Creamsicle Meltdown

Us dealers, we had nicknames for many of the casino's regulars, but not nicknames we used to their faces. Mrs. Dyson, who always wore about a pound of rhinestones, was Mrs. DeBeers. Mr. McIlvoy, the fat guy, we called Hamburger, as in Big Mac. Mr. Lee was Super-Split because he split whenever he had two of the same cards, whether or not it was a good play. Not every regular had a nickname. We didn't have one for Mr. Sundberg, who played smart and was a good tipper.

Then there was Pauly Bolinger, Creamsicle, who always wore a pale orange sports coat and a white shirt. You could count on Pauly to come in once a month with a big stake. You could count on him to start out playing smart, never splitting his cards on tens, always doubling his bet on eleven. And he'd keep playing smart if he got ahead, so that on some rare nights he'd go home having tripled his stake. More often, though, his play would become impulsive as soon as he had a run of losses. Then you could count on him to do stupid things like split tens with the dealer showing eight, counting on luck to bring him nines or tens. Which it usually didn't, of course.

I didn't like Creamsicle. He didn't tip. On nights when he lost everything but his cab fare home he'd cry and tell me how he lived in a trailer at the edge of the desert. When things like that happened, it was my job to stand at my station and say, "Better luck next time, Mr. Bolinger." For regulars at the high stakes tables, if they weren't staying in our hotel, we could offer them a limo ride home. But Creamsicle wasn't enough of a high roller for that. He played the five-dollar table. So I'd have to stay at my station, keep dealing to the other players, and endure his tears until the pit boss noticed and had him escorted. Gently, of course, so as not to offend him, but firmly, so that other players at the table wouldn't feel too bad or think too much and change their minds about what they were doing with their money.

I liked it best when Creamsicle won, even though he didn't tip. Tears at the blackjack table, they're no fun for anybody.

My last night on the floor of the casino, Creamsicle came in late in my shift and joined two other players at my table. He played even for a while, up a couple hundred dollars, down a couple. He was down and had lost several hands in a row when I dealt him a four and a six. Ten. The house's hand showed a five. The smart thing to do in that situation is to double your bet. That's what Creamsicle did. It was the right play, but it didn't work out. He lost. I couldn't have told you that this particular disappointment would be his turning point, but his pile of chips was shrinking, so he was headed for one of his bad nights. Sure enough, after that hand he played with more hope than strategy. He started to make bigger bets, more reckless bets. He lost faster.

On his last bet of fifty dollars—it should have been his last bet—I dealt him a pair of eights. The house showed a six.

I waited. The player to his left said, "What's it going to be?"

Creamsicle rubbed his forehead. He wanted to split those eights, which ordinarily would have been the smartest bet. But it would mean putting another fifty dollars on the table. I knew that the only money he had left would be the fifty he kept in his breast pocket for cab fare. The one thing Creamsicle had going for him, the only thing I liked about him, was that he never would bet his ride home.

He didn't split the eights. He stood on sixteen, and under the circumstances, it was the right thing to do, or at least the thing I wanted him to do. I didn't want to see him bet his cab fare. But I dealt the house seventeen. He lost.

He put both hands on the felt. "Fuck me," he said. He stood up.

Neither of the other players looked at him. His eyes were red-rimmed and turning watery.

I said, "Better luck next time, Mr. Bolinger."

"Fuck that." He took the fifty out of his orange breast pocket and put it on the table.

I looked at him. I looked at the pit boss, whose attention was elsewhere for the moment. I looked at Pauly Bolinger. *Pick it up,* I was thinking. *Pick it up, and put it back in your pocket.*

He didn't meet my gaze. I did my job. I slotted the bill and gave him his chips. He pushed them forward and proceeded to hit on twelve. The house showed ten, so he was at least playing smart, even if I thought he shouldn't be playing at all. He drew a ten card. Twenty-two. Busted.

He pushed his chair back in a fury. "I'm an idiot!"

The pit boss was looking our way, reaching into his pocket to transmit a signal.

"Take it easy, Mr. Bolinger," I said.

"Right," he said. "Take it easy. Better luck next time." He made fists. "Why do I do this?"

The pit boss came around behind Pauly, and across the floor I could see a broad-shouldered Dark Suit starting our way.

Pauly slapped the table. "Fuck me!"

Players around the room were looking at him, except for the two players at my table. They were looking anywhere but at Pauly. The pit boss put his hand on Pauly's shoulder.

I stepped back a little from my table and showed my empty hands to the boss and to the security cameras. I reached into my breast pocket. I wasn't supposed to do that. Once tips went in, they weren't supposed to come out again while the dealer was at the table. I found two twenty-five dollar chips. I rapped them on the table, then pushed them at Pauly.

"What's this?" He blinked. I could see his anger finding a new target. "I don't want your—"

"It's a stake."

The pit boss gave me a dark look.

"I'm staking you one hand," I said to Pauly. "You win, you go home."

"You can't do that," said the pit boss. "You can't have a stake in a game you're dealing."

"Right," I said. "It's a gift then. Play it or cash it, Mr. Bolinger."

"And if I lose?" said Pauly.

"Too bad."

"I don't owe you?"

"I said it's a gift."

The boss frowned at me, and I could see that he didn't like this but couldn't quite decide whether to shut down my table right then. He probably should have. But what he did was take his hand off of Pauly's shoulder and let him sit down. The other two players were watching me, like this was the most interesting thing that had happened all night. I gestured to the Dark Suit, waving him off. He kept coming toward us, but at an easier pace.

To the other two players, I said, "Place your bets."

In that hand, Pauly stood on seventeen with a dealer six showing. Good. The house busted with twenty-four.

I paid Pauly's bet. He slid me fifty in chips—the first time he ever tipped me, and it was with my own money. I rapped the chips on the table, showed them to Dark Suit and the pit boss since they were right there, and put them in my pocket. "Good night, Mr. Bolinger," I said.

He nodded. He stood up, straightened his lapels, and left.

"Your shift's over," the pit boss said, and he told the remaining players that my table was closed. His cell phone rang. Before he answered it, he said, "I bet someone upstairs wants a word with you."

I had been in Mr. Janes's office only once before, when I was hired. Mr. Janes watched me come in without saying a word. He gestured with one hand for me to sit down. The other hand held an unlit cigar.

"Want to tell me what was that about?" said Mr. Janes. "You couldn't stand to see the Creamsicle melt?"

"I don't know, sir."

"I think you do know. I sure as hell think I know."

"All right."

He pointed at me. "Your tips don't come out of your pocket while you're at your table."

"I know, sir."

"I could fire you for that."

"Yes, Mr. Janes. I know."

"You know. You know." He put the cigar down and folded his hands. "Well, I'm not going to fire you for that. You're an arrogant motherfucker, aren't you?"

"No, sir."

"You want to keep your job?"

"Yes, sir."

"Good. Otherwise there would be no satisfaction in firing your ass." He squinted at me. "I've been in the business for thirty years. Thirty fucking years. Do you think it's easy? Do you think I just count my money and sleep like a baby? Guys like Creamsicle, I see them every day. Do you think I never once asked myself what the fuck I was doing?"

I just looked at him, and he looked back at me. "I'm not sure I know what you're saying."

"You're fired," he said, "and don't think for a minute that I feel sorry for you, because I most certainly do not. Guys like Creamsicle I have to look at every day, but with a guy like you, I have a choice."

So I was fired. So what? I could have been dealing blackjack someplace else in a week, no problem. And some days I miss the money. Nobody ever tips me two hundred dollars for bringing their salad and sirloin. I do miss that part. The money was great, and I was used to guys like Creamsicle. I had learned to take it, even if I did cave a little that one time. But inside every Casino, there's a Mr. Janes. Inside every casino, there's a guy with plenty of time to think about the business he's in, but he's got a good life. So he's careful. He doesn't put anything but money on the table. That's the part I couldn't live with any more.

Donat Bobet's Halloween

Donat Bobet invited me to his home for the night of Halloween. I came as a pirate, a costume which I assembled out of a bandana and the cardboard spool from a roll of paper towels. I tied the bandana on my head. Before I stuck the cardboard tube into my belt, I wrote on it with bold, piratical letters: *Wooden Sword.* I considered whether or not to write on my face with a black marker the words *False Beard.* I decided against it. I had work the next day, and the ink might not come off.

I arrived a little after the appointed hour. I knocked on the poet's door, expecting that the party would already be underway. To my surprise, when Donat opened the door to his rooms, he was entirely alone.

"Am I the first?" I said.

He looked puzzled. "The first?" Then he saw my sword. "Ah! No! I should have explained myself," he said. "This is no party for the grown-ups. For me, Halloween is an affair entirely for the children! I meant only that you might come and help me with the candy!"

"Oh."

"And you have gone to the trouble of making a costume! A very fine one, too!"

"You can tell what I am, then?"

"My friend, do you think I do not have eyes in my head? But one moment!" There were colored pens on his dining table, and small squares of paper, many with writing and drawing on them. He took up a blank piece and wrote on it in red: *Scarlet Macaw*. He pinned the bird to my shoulder. "There!"

"Thank you," I said.

"That pulls it all together, I think."

"And what sort of candy will we be giving the children?"

"I'm afraid that I have eaten it all," Donat confessed. "There is nothing to give them but the wrappers." He picked up three of the squares of paper and gave them to me.

The first, with a red and yellow design, said Sugar Bomb. "Ingredients: Raw sugar, corn syrup, maltose, dextrose, fructose, sucrose, brown sugar, gunpowder, BANG!"

The second, with a blue moon and white stars against a black background, was called Space Dust. "Ingredients: Carbon, hydrogen, oxygen, nitrogen, calcium, phosphorus, sulfur. May contain traces of the rings of Saturn."

The third candy wrapper was for Dead Poet Yummy. "Ingredients: Spun sugar and air. Some of the air in this candy was once breathed by Jean Genet. Swallow it whole and then write a poem about stealing, you little thief!"

"But," I said, "aren't the children disappointed?"

"Ah, the children," said Donat Bobet. "They never come."

Border Crossing

Lately I don't recognize this country, the land of my birth. The contours of the land are the same. I can buy what I always bought in the stores. The weather has changed, though. Last winter, we had no snow, but the wind blew love letters to dead soldiers into drifts up to my knees.

When I drove north across the border, I didn't have smuggling on my mind. I drove through the mountains like any tourist who wanted only a little respite. In the alpine snow fields, I saw blue shadows. That particular color has its own name, a name unknown on my side of the border.

The border guard walked around my car, inspecting with a mirror on a long rod. He made me open the trunk. A dog sniffed the upholstery. "Take off your shoes," the guard said. With gloved fingers, he lifted the insole to find the word I had hidden underneath, the word for blue shadows in snow. He said, "Did you think we wouldn't know where to look?"

When I was a boy of five, I played all summer in a green jumpsuit with insignia on the sleeves, firing my cap guns at the enemy trees. I had a red fireman's helmet, too, with the long brim in back, and I was spanked for aiming the garden hose through an open bedroom window. When I grew up, I was going to be a fireman or a soldier, and I didn't see much difference between them.

Across the border, the money is more colorful. On the blue or red bills are portraits of heros whose names I never heard in school.

Lately I don't recognize this country, the land of my birth. These mountains are the same mountains. The presidents on my money are the same ones whose names I learned in school. The weather has changed, though. Last winter, we had no snow. Instead, the names of dead presidents fell from the sky. Wind blew the black letters of *WASHINGTON* and *LINCOLN* into drifts up to my knees.

It was no trouble at all to cross the border. The guard looked at my passport and stamped it only because I asked her to. I wanted some physical sign that I had been somewhere else, some evidence besides memory.

Certainly, I did not have smuggling on my mind. On my second day there, I drove across the grasslands at first light. Cresting a rise, I saw wheat fields lying before me like a blanket. We have such fields in my own country, but we do not have a word for the color of the ripe grain first thing in the morning.

The border guard walked around my car, inspecting with a mirror on a long rod. He made me open the trunk. A dog sniffed the upholstery. "Open your mouth," he said. With gloved fingers, he lifted my tongue to find the word I had hidden underneath, the word for miles of ripe wheat in the morning light. He said, "Did you think we wouldn't know where to look?"

There is a border between innocence and experience, a border that moves. I keep thinking that I have crossed it, and having crossed it, I change my mind about what I know. I am a man now, and I know what it is to be a man. But then I find that the border has moved ahead of me, and I still have much to learn about being a man. War is never necessary, I think. But the border has moved. War is sometimes necessary. No, I find that I am still on the side of innocence.

The same trees grow on either side of the border. In the other country, many people speak the same language as the language they speak in the country of my birth. Not all the words are the same. The dust doesn't know which country it belongs to. Wind blows dust north today and south tomorrow, increasing one nation at the expense of the other, then taking back what it gave.

Lately I don't recognize this country, even though the trees are the same on either side of the border. My own country feels strange. It is the other side that feels familiar. Familiar, and strange at the same time. In the land of my birth, the weather is still the weather, although last winter we went without snow.

For miles and miles, no fence divides one side from the other. You could walk back and forth all day, testing the difference until night fell. You might wake to find your head in one country and your feet in the other.

In fact, I did not walk the unguarded portions of the border at night, but when I was in the other country, I walked beyond the glow of my campfire until I could no longer see my hand before my face. I lay on my back and looked up through the trees silhouetted against the starry sky. The darkness between the stars is the same darkness we see from my own country.

The border guard walked around my car, writing notes

on a clipboard. He made me pop the hood and open the trunk. He took me to a room without windows. "Take off your shirt," he said. He used a sharp blade on the skin of my chest, and he peeled back my skin to reveal the word I had hidden underneath, the word for the dark between the stars. He said, "Did you think we wouldn't know where to look?"

In the other country, they wear red plastic poppies on their lapels to remember the war dead.

In the mountains of the other country, I came upon a field of poppies. They were not red at all, but a shade of orange.

Lately I don't recognize this country, the land of my birth. I feel sometimes as if I crossed a border that I hadn't intended to cross. Those are the hills that have always been there, forested with trees that I know. But last winter, we had no snow, and the wind blew the dried petals of poppies into drifts up to my knees.

The border guard walked around my car. He inspected the back seat, the trunk, the hubcaps. He took me to a room without windows. "Take off your shirt," he said. He pushed a needle into my arm and drew out my blood. He spread the blood on a plate of glass. He read the word that I was smuggling home. He said, "Did you think we wouldn't know where to look?"

Fish Out of Water

I am good at this. Just now, I have reeled in a steelhead trout. I scoop it up with my net and walk up the bank to where I keep the rest of my catch. Things I have fished out of the river: boots and shoes in good condition, belts, a suit and tie, dress shirts, assorted kitchenware, an air-conditioner, a Bible, a piano, two televisions, a motorcycle, a four-door sedan with only 35,000 miles on the odometer, a four-bedroom house, a wife, a son, and a daughter. I hold up the steelhead. "Dinner for my family of four!" I say.

My son won't look me in the eye. "It's catch and release," he says.

"I know it's catch and release," I say. "Everybody knows it's catch and release." Actually, I have been so busy fishing that I forgot.

"We're not yours," says my daughter.

"Is today a day of special rudeness?" I say. "No one is anyone's. Everyone knows that." But this, too, is one of the things that had slipped my mind while I was busy casting, reeling, and netting. I had forgotten all about tossing everything back. The truth is, I don't want to throw everything back. I am good at fishing.

I return to the water's edge and cast my line again. Fishing helps me to forget my troubles, but now I see the sign that is posted in the middle of the river. EVERYTHING OF WATER RETURNS TO THE RIVER.

There is still time for more catching before I have to release, I think. Besides, is a house of water? Is a sedan of water? Are my land-dwelling wife and children of water?

I reel in my line and find that the river has taken my bait and given me nothing in return. That happens. I reach into my bait bucket for some bait and mold an attractive piece of desire around my hook. I cast out again.

My wife comes to stand next to me. I don't like it when she's so close to the water. Ripples pulse as if the water were reaching for her. "How about that fish?" I say. "Isn't it nearly time for dinner?" But she just stands there, looking into the current.

"Look," I say to the river. "Let's make a deal." I reel in my line. "Let me keep what I have, and I will be without desire." I turn over my bait bucket and dump the contents into the water.

"To be without desire is also a desire," says my wife. Sure enough, the bucket is not quite empty. I crouch next to the current and fill the bucket with water. I swirl water in the bucket. I dump water from the bucket. The bucket is still not empty, and now my hands are wet and dripping. Water drips from my fingers, and then something not water. Something pink. I realize that it is my fingers themselves, melting away and dripping back into the river.

Something Is in the Air

1. What Is This New World?

The vole's life has changed. The snow through which it had always tunneled has vanished. Seeds that it finds along the ground now are swollen plump, or sweetly sprouting. Snails have emerged, slow protein that is easy to catch. New perfumes rise from black earth. Green shoots show where to dig for bulbs. New neighbors arrive, some unseen. The first northern harrier home from its migration hovers, hovers, dives.

2. Harbingers

He would tell his daughter to look up from the screen of her phone, but he doesn't want to earn another scowl. Trees in the mall parking lot have opened chartreuse leaves, too young to be green. Golden insects dance in the afternoon light. He leaves his jacket in the car, walks with her. Inside the mall, she sees yellow espadrilles in a shop window. "Sandals," she says. "Springtime!"

3. Evictions

As a young homeowner, he knocked wasp nests from under the eaves. Against his wife's protest, he nailed tight a loose soffit, sealing the starlings inside. This spring a family of nutria have burrowed beneath his porch. They're gnawing the joists, but he lets them stay. Gone soft, thinks his daughter, in memory of Mom's tender heart. But, no, he just knows at last that he is a tenant.

Grave Goods

During the night, the river had exhaled a fog so dense that as I looked out from my kitchen window, I could barely detect the glow of windows across the street. Winter had been especially dark and gray in Montreal, and now, just as the trees were beginning to bud, this further grayness was particularly cruel.

It was Saturday. I put on my coat and went to the apartment of Donat Bobet. I told myself that as the constitution of poets was delicate, if I hungered for sunshine, he must be starved for it. He answered the door, yawning and blinking away sleep, in a tattered cotton bathrobe upon which he had written the word SILK.

"Good morning!" I said with more cheer than I felt. "A gray plague lies over the city. I am on my way to Mount Royal to see if, perhaps, I can walk to the sun. Will you join me?"

"Walk to the sun?" he said. "That is tens of millions of miles." He frowned. "I will need my good shoes." Once he had dressed, I took him to a café so that he might have some breakfast. While Donat ate, I gazed out the window and found myself hoping that the fog would not burn off before we had seen whether we could escape it.

In an hour, we were on Mount Royal, walking in the cemetery. The fog was more persistent than I had imagined.

Even at such an elevation, we had not risen above the gray, and we could see only those monuments closest to us. The rest receded into silhouettes and shadows.

The world felt silent and empty. "These must be the right conditions for meeting a ghost," I said.

"The ghosts you meet in a graveyard are not the interesting ones," said Donat.

"Oh?" I said. "And why is that?"

"Interesting ghosts have things to do. Only mad ghosts are reliably found at a grave."

"Mad ghosts?"

"In this very cemetery, for instance, there is a ghost who in life utterly opposed any supernatural phenomena. He lies perfectly still, hovering horizontally above his grave, refusing to speak or even to open his eyes." The poet shook his head. "No. Like us, most ghosts come to graves only as visitors."

I gave a little laugh. "And how do you know this?"

Donat shot me a glare that told me that he knew what he knew, and that I had better not begin to insult him with logic.

From ahead of us on the path came a scraping sound, as if of metal on stone. "Could that be one?" I said. "A ghost?"

Now Donat looked at me with an expression of extreme patience. "No," he said. And shapes emerged from the fog. Two people worked at a headstone. We drew near enough to see a man and a woman. The man was scraping moss from the granite, and the woman bathed the scraped stone using a sponge and a bucket of water.

When we walked on far enough so as not to be overheard,

I said, "Do you suppose the dead care about such attention to their graves?"

Apparently this question was not worthy of a reply. We walked on in silence until Donat stopped at the grave of a child. A high curb surrounded the grave. The ground within the curb was filled with colored spheres, which I soon recognized as marbles. A teddy bear rested on the curb, leaning against the headstone. I applied the usual subtraction of one date from the other. By my calculation, this little boy had died before he was five, ten years ago.

"This is sad," said Donat.

"Indeed," I agreed. "To die so young. To lose a child..."

"Yes, yes," Donat said. "That, too. But look at the bear. It has not been in the weather long. It is new." He looked at me. "This scene touches my sympathies."

"The poor parents," I said. "Ten years, and it is still a fresh injury to them."

"This is a wrong that we must right," Donat said. He seized me by the elbow and began to march me out of the cemetery.

"What can we do?" I said. "What can we possibly do?"

But the poet was in the power of his passion. He would not answer me until we had left the environs of the cemetery, and then he only said, "A corner store. We must find a corner store."

We did. Donat gave me a shopping basket to hold while he searched the shelves for what he needed. Six beers. A sandwich. Three cigars. Matches. He lingered in the "Men's Interest" section of the magazines until he found one called

Lingerie, which he flipped through quickly. I could tell as the pictures went by that it was a magazine largely devoid of text. "Yes," he pronounced. "This will do." He looked at me. "I hope you won't mind paying. I'm afraid that I did not prepare myself for meeting such urgent expenses during our walk."

I have never minded supplying Donat Bobet with food or drink. I confess that the magazine embarrassed me, for both our sakes, but to refuse meant I must explain my objection. I paid.

Donat took up our purchases in one arm, grabbed my elbow again, and we retraced our steps. Before long we stood once more before the grave. The fog had thinned a little, but still afforded privacy for the three of us: myself, Donat, and the grave. Donat gave me a cigar, took two for himself, and lit all three. One of these he laid on top of the headstone. He opened three beers, gave me one, and set the second on the grave. He began to drink from the third.

I did not understand, and said so. Donat held up his hand. All would be revealed. He took the magazine from the paper sack and walked around the grave, pulling at his face as if solving a difficult problem. Finally, he knelt beside the headstone and proceeded to wedge the magazine between that stone and the curb. He pulled the magazine out again, folded it, and this time managed to make it disappear from view altogether. "So his mother won't find it," he said. He met my gaze. "They still think of him as a dead boy. But it has been ten years. He is becoming a dead man."

"Aha," I said. I puffed on my cigar, appreciating now that I smoked in the company of a ghost. I clinked my beer bottle against the bottle on the grave. I drank.

Later, as we walked home, fog still obscured the sky. "We did not manage to walk all the way to the sun," Donat said, "but we accomplished something of significance." The bag he carried contained two empty bottles, three full ones, and...

"What about the sandwich?" I said.

"Naturally the sandwich," said Donat Bobet, "is my lunch."

Halcyon Night

His daughter was about to turn eighteen and leave home for college, but even at twelve years old she had already moved into a distant orbit. He had an idea for her birthday, but no confidence that it would matter to her. Things had been easier when she was small. He and his wife had arranged their teaching and observatory hours so that one of them could be home with her most days. When his daughter was six or seven, he could excite her interest in things by being excited about them himself. In their home laboratory, they made a vinegar-and-baking-soda volcano, examined onion cells under the microscope, built a pinhole camera. They caught horned toads with their hands and made a desert terrarium. At ten, she could name the constellations and their major stars. But by the time she started seventh grade, she was wearing lipstick and knew the brand names of clothes. She knew all about movie stars and other things that didn't matter.

"That happens to girls," said his wife.

"Did it happen to you?"

"I was different. She's normal."

The official birthday present would be something his daughter wanted. His wife could see to that. He would give her something he wanted her to want. "A fire balloon," he told his daughter. "I've never actually seen one. It's a hot air balloon on a small scale. We can build it out of tissue paper and balsa. Birthday candles supply the heat. We could drive into the desert and launch it on the night of your birthday."

"Dad," she said, drawing out the syllable as if she needed to speak slowly for him. "I have plans? On the night of my birthday I'm going to have a party? With my friends?"

"It doesn't have to be on your birthday. How about the next night?"

"Don't you think I'm a little old for that stuff?"

"It's for me, too."

"So it's for you."

"All right," he said. "I'll build it. For me. You can come watch me launch it on the day after your birthday. If you feel like it. If you aren't too busy."

"Don't be like that."

"How am I being?"

"All I'm saying is that I'm not a kid."

A week before her birthday, he bought beige tissue paper and tiny paintbrushes for the glue. He built a platform for the birthday candles out of balsa. After dinner one night, he cut out eight triangles of tissue paper for the top and bottom, four rectangles for the sides. He laid the pieces out on the floor of his study, and started to brush glue onto the seams.

From the doorway, his daughter said, "That's the color you're making it?"

"We're probably not going to be able to recover it. I want it to blend in wherever it goes down."

"It's boring."

He kept gluing. "If we were making this together, you could choose the colors."

"That's okay. I'm going out."

After she had gone, he left the balloon half finished and went to look at the colors of her bedroom.

She was out right until the very last minute before her curfew that night, as she was for each of the following nights.

The night of her birthday, he and his wife agreed to extend the daughter's curfew to one in the morning. Not that they'd know if she were out a little later than that. They each had telescope time and lab meetings at the observatory. His lasted until two.

His daughter still wasn't home when he got there a little before three. In the morning, his wife was sleeping beside him, and his daughter's bedroom door was locked. Both slept until noon. He decided not to ask questions or lay down the law. The girl was eighteen, after all.

When she came to the kitchen in her robe and poured herself some cereal, he showed her the four foot tall tissue-paper balloon. It was red and lilac.

"Much better," she said. Here eyes were bloodshot.

"Launch tonight?"

She closed her eyes and nodded gently.

His wife told her research assistants to carry on without her for one night. She wanted to be there for the launch. As a family, they drove the highway far enough to escape the city lights, and then on a dirt road far enough to escape the lights of cars.

"Perfect conditions," his wife said as they stepped out into the darkness. "I don't feel any breeze at all."

"A halcyon night," he said.

"What?" said the daughter.

"A halcyon night. A still night," he said.

"I don't think that's what halcyon means."

"It means kingfisher time."

"What are you talking about?"

"The ancient Greeks never saw a kingfisher nest. So they reasoned that the birds must be building their nests and laying their eggs somewhere out of sight. On the open sea."

"This has something to do with halcyon?"

"*Alkuon.* That was their word for kingfisher. They thought that the birds had the power to make the wind stop blowing for a few days so they could build their nests and hatch their chicks at sea. *Alkuon*, halcyon. Halcyon days. Perfect weather."

"Where do kingfishers really lay their eggs?" said the daughter.

"In burrows."

"You know the weirdest stuff."

"I do," he said.

"The Greeks were lame."

"They had a theory that fit the available evidence. There are some pretty strange things about biology that are true." Such as life happening at all, he thought. Such as life giving rise to consciousness. Such as daughters.

He had her hold the red LED flashlight so he could see what he was doing without ruining his night vision. His wife helped him unfold the balloon and hold it upright. He lit a match, squinting against the brightness. One by one, he lit the birthday candles.

"Shall we sing happy birthday?" he said.

His daughter said, "Let's not."

Her parents sang anyway. Light from the candles made the whole balloon glow. Hot air made it plump.

"It's beautiful, Dad."

His wife said, "Ready?"

They let go. In two heartbeats, the fire balloon was over their heads. It rose faster than he expected. Faster than he would have liked. Too soon, the glow of the canopy was too faint to see. The candle flames glowed as an orange point of light, getting farther and farther away and just beginning to drift down range in a high-elevation breeze.

"Wow," the daughter said. "It looks like Ophiuchus has a new star."

He smiled.

The orange point flickered. It vanished. The candles had burned themselves out.

"Aw," his daughter said. "It's kind of sad. You make something beautiful like that, and then it's gone."

In the darkness, he felt for his wife's hand.

BONUS STORIES

Donat Bobet, Exterminator

Some features of my apartment building are rather old fashioned, and among these is the intercom system. A visitor in the lobby may press a button to ring my apartment, and as long as the button is pressed, my bell continues to ring. Most of my friends ring once, discreetly. *Brrring.* A few ring twice, to make certain. *Brrring. Bring.*

One Saturday morning not long ago, someone leaned on the button as if my building were on fire. *Brrrrrrrrrrrrrring. Ring-ring-ring. Brrrrrrrrrrrrring. Ring-ring-ring. Brrrrrrrrrrrrring. Ring-ring-ring.*

I picked up my receiver and demanded, "Who is this?"

A man's voice said, "Catastrophe! Disaster! Utter ruin and devastation! I am almost without hope!"

I recognized the voice and the drama. "What is it, Donat?" I tried to keep from sounding too skeptical, for the poet's lamentations would likely sound precisely the same if he had bad news from the doctor or another rejection slip from Écrits des Forges.

"Infestation!" he said. "My apartment is in a terrible state! Please, let me enlist your aid!"

I buzzed him in, and while waiting for him to ascend, I wondered what sort of creatures could be infesting the poet's apartment. His cupboards were ususally bare. A family of mice that tried to live on Donat's surplus would be poor indeed.

When I opened the door to him, Donat clutched his hair in both fists. "I cannot think! I cannot work! I cannot produce! A man of ideas cannot live like this!" There were dark circles under his eyes, but they were a bit smudged at the edges, suggesting makeup.

"You say your apartment is infested?"

"With termites!"

That sounded troubling until I considered, what would they eat? The furniture? Donat's apartment building was made of steel and concrete. Some trace of disbelief must have revealed itself in my expression.

"No, not ordinary termites," said Donat. "Those I could deal with. Pass the hat for funds, call the exterminator, problem solved. That class of termites is easy to deal with. My friend, I am speaking of..." He trailed off to a whisper, as if he hardly dared to say the words aloud. "Termites of the imagination."

I laughed.

"Oh, you think it's funny? Haven't you heard me? It is impossible for me to conceive of a single line, to conjure an image, to arrive at a metaphor! Why? Because where termites of the ordinary class devour wood, termites of the imagination feast upon... ideas!"

"I'm sorry," I said. "That does sound serious."

"I need your help, your immediate assistance. Infestations of this kind are not easily remedied. If you are my friend, if you are, as I believe you to be, a true patron of the arts, you must help me, beginning tonight, to enact those measures that will destroy the colony."

"I am," I said, "at your service."

"You must clear your social calendar for the next two Saturdays, in case of escalation!" He drew a pen and paper from his pocket and began to write down instructions. "You must call your friends and mine! Anyone with a music collection who can also contribute a hot dish! But it's not just any music that we want!"

So it fell to me to arrange a pot-luck dinner at Donat's apartment that very night. I asked guests to bring a bottle of wine, a dish to share, and determination to help the poet rid his apartment of imaginary termites. Oh, and each guest was also invited to bring a CD of the most ludicrous pop music he or she owned.

"The first line of defense," Donat proclaimed to his assembled guests, "is to starve the termites. My friends, while we dine, we will listen to loud pop music, music which is generally devoid of ideas and which, played at sufficient volume, also renders thought impossible. The objective tonight, everyone, is to have no ideas!"

I could see at once, as Donat's little stereo began to play a medley of girl bands, that this plan was doomed to failure. Guests began to argue about whether various pop songs really were devoid of ideas. One woman grew incensed when she saw that another guest's choice of meaningless pop was an album by Avril Lavigne. She cried, "Are you mad? Or are you a pig?"

"People are still thinking," I observed to Donat as he put away some pot luck portions in his refrigerator.

"Alas," he agreed. "We will have to escalate!"

Donat hosted another pot luck extermination party the following Saturday. This time he instructed me to tell guests to bring along political manifestos, depressed moods, memories of former lovers... Anything, in short, that contained or would help them to generate poisonous thoughts. "We'll let the termites eat their fill of foul ideas!" Donat pledged. Guests were also asked to bring a bottle of wine and a hot dish.

As a party, this was not among the most pleasant evenings I have passed with Donat and his assembled patrons, perhaps because Donat circulated throughout the night, interrupting conversations to ask if there were not, perhaps, an ugly side to the story someone was telling. He made an effort to inject some racism, some sexism, or some national pride into any subject that came up. The guests were rather subdued and grumpy, and some left without remembering to claim their leftovers.

Was the evening a success? Donat seemed hopeful. "There was definitely poison in the air." He found that some of the wine bottles had not even been opened. "A success, yes. But a total success? We shall see."

When Donat did not call me during the week to arrange a third attempt, I guessed that the imaginary termites had been exterminated. But I was wrong. On Saturday afternoon, my bell rang. Once. Politely. *Brring.*

"Hello?" I said into the receiver.

"My dear friend," came a weary sounding reply. "I have executed the last resort."

"Donat?"

"Let me in," he said, "and I will tell you the sorry tale."

When I opened my apartment door some minutes later, I met a stoop-shouldered poet. He was covered in white dust. His hair was full of it, his clothes spattered with it, his face whitened so that his eyes were like holes poked in the snow.

"Donat!" I said. "What happened?"

"Pardon me?" said the poet. "You'll have to speak up. My ears are still ringing." Pinned to his shoulder was a slip of paper with something written on it. White dust obscured the writing. I brushed at the dust, which proved to be flour. The slip of paper said, "Splinter of wood." Pinned in the crook of Donat's elbow was another slip that read, "Rubble."

I ushered him in solicitously. I offered him a seat, not minding that I would have to vacuum later the Donat-shaped impression he would leave behind in flour.

"Dynamite," he said wearily. "The last resort. My neighbors and I are all homeless now."

"That's terrible!"

"We will rebuild. We will be a testimony to the human spirit."

"I'm sure."

He managed a little smile. "But this is a victory! He patted his chest, raising a white cloud. "We will rebuild, and the new instance of my apartment will be without termites! I'll be able to write again!"

"Can I get you something?" I said. "Do you want some water?"

He laughed. "Water?" he said. "Did Caesar have water when he returned from his campaigns?" He shook his head. "No, my friend, we have done the difficult thing, the brave thing, at great cost. We must mark the occasion with champagne! With a fine dinner! And for once, it will be my treat!"

I thanked him for his generosity, even though I was sure that after we made reservations, he would discover, to his horror, that he must have inadvertently blown his money, every last cent, to smithereens.

—*Bruce Holland Rogers and Muse*

The Yellow House

Dullenty, worn down by three broken marriages, by a bad pension, by his doctor's sour admonitions, decided to go home. He had worked hard as a young man to get out of Townsend, Montana, but now the place seemed to suit him again. Even in his reduced circumstances, he could afford to buy a house in Townsend. Summers, he could take a boat out all day on Canyon Ferry Lake or play nine holes for ten dollars on the Old Baldy course. Winters, he'd stay in and read or do a little wood working.

At one time, moving back to Townsend would have felt like a defeat, but by now almost anyone who would have received Dullenty's return with a sneer was dead or had moved away. Scott Orr was still around, and Dullenty planned to look him up, but Dullenty's best childhood friend had died in Korea. Other friends had moved away for jobs in livelier corners of the country, their distant addresses lost with the Christmas-card list that one ex-wife or another used to maintain.

Moving back wasn't a defeat, but it threatened to make Dullenty feel even more diminished if he didn't handle it just right. That's why he resisted the first house the real estate agent showed him, even though it fit every criterion he had named. The house was modest, had a small yard that would be easy to maintain, had been modernized and updated only about a decade ago. The problem was, Dullenty knew that house, and for him it was a sad, sorry place.

"The Hockingberry family lived here," he told the agent.

She looked at the papers inside her folder. "The current owner's name is Marks."

"But to me," Dullenty said, "this is the Hockingberry house." He didn't tell the agent what that meant to him, but he remembered his mother instructing him to steer clear of the Hockingberry kids. The one girl, Shirley, was a cripple, and Dullenty's mother didn't want him catching polio, even though lots of people said Shirley couldn't use her legs because of a birth defect, not because of any disease you could catch. She had spina bifida, they said.

Dullenty heeded his mother's warning and didn't make friends with Earl Hockingberry, who was about his age. He'd see the crippled girl on the way to school, but she was easy to avoid. She'd be with her younger sister, Joan, who pulled her to school in a wagon, or on a sled in winter, right down the middle of the road.

Now, walking the rooms of the old house, Dullenty felt a double sorrow. On one hand, he thought of the six Hockingberry kids crowded together with their parents in these small rooms, of the disappointment that must have attended Shirley's birth, of the diminished life for the sister who had to haul her around. On the other hand, he felt the sorrow of shame. He had allowed his mother's fears to dictate. And his wasn't the only family that shunned the Hockingberrys.

"I don't think I can live in this house," he said.

The agent asked for no explanation. The Hockingberry house was the cheapest on her list, so it would have meant a small commission. She seemed happy to move on to the next address, a bigger house on a bigger lot, or the third property for sale, which was bigger still.

Unfortunately, those other places were just too much house for Dullenty to live in alone. It would cost a fortune to heat them, and what would he do with those extra rooms?

Townsend was not the sort of place where property came on the market often. There were only four houses for sale, and only the old Hockingberry place was the right size. Dullenty decided on a course of action. He bought the house, and he exorcised it of its old sorrows. He painted the rooms yellow, and the outside an even brighter yellow. He washed away his memories of the Hockingberrys with color. He worked with brush and roller, slow work, but it was a small house, and doing the work by hand helped make him intimate with the space, helped him think about his past, helped him make peace with his regrets. He was sorry he'd shunned the Hockingberrys. Maybe some of them still lived. Not Shirley, the cripple, surely. She'd been kept out of school a lot, was sickly even as a child. But maybe her sister. Maybe there was still someone he could apologize to.

With the work of painting, Dullenty felt some of his taste for living return. From his little yard, he inspected his handiwork and appreciated the lemony brilliance of his gutters and eaves against the immense and intense blue of Montana sky. Maybe these later years would be all right.

Dullenty sent for his furniture. Then he called Scott Orr.

"I was wondering when I'd hear from you," Orr said. He knew all about Dullenty, that he'd been staying at the Mustang Motel, that he'd bought the Hockingberrys' old house, that he had painted it yellow. Dullenty had forgotten about how news traveled in Townsend.

They met for drinks at the Fish Tale Tavern. By drinks, it turned out that they meant soda water for Orr and coffee for Dullenty. They talked in turns about the workout each man had given his liver in his younger years, and then about the people they had grown up with. Eventually, Dullenty found himself talking about the Hockingberrys. He said it was such a shame that the town had been so hard on them, particularly on Shirley. He imagined that she hadn't had much of a life.

"You don't think Shirley Hockingberry had much of a life?" said Orr. "You mean, former Mayor Hockingberry? The woman who still gives fiddle lessons out of her home? That same Shirley Hockingberry?" The Hockingberrys were some of the sturdiest stock in Broadwater County, Orr said. Yes, all of Shirley's brothers and sisters were still alive, though they all lived elsewhere. He named names: Walt in a rest home in Helena. Earl in good shape in Denver. Joan running a business in Albuquerque. Will and Patricia fine, as far as Orr knew. And Shirley was right here in Townsend. Orr could take Dullenty to see her if he liked.

"She wouldn't know me," Dullenty said. He thought he might like to talk to her one day, but he'd have to think about what to say.

"I'll swing you by her place when we're finished here," Orr said. And that's how Dullenty found himself in Orr's rig an hour later, pulling up in front of a house on Harrison

Avenue. There was a small fenced yard. Three little dogs came shooting out of a doggy door, yapping happily at Orr's truck. The van parked behind the electric gate sported a hydraulic lift. The thing that most caught Dullenty's attention, though, the thing that made him smile, was the color of the house: bright and cheerful, full of zest, almost giving off the smell of lemons.

Everything Must Go

Christoph wrote letters to his son and two daughters saying, "Whatever you want that was your mother's or mine, whatever you have seen for sale in the shop and craved for your own, come collect it by the end of March, or at least tell me what it is and I will ship it to you." Then each of his children called in turn to ask what was wrong. Was he ill?

He was fine, he told them. He was just lightening the load, and whatever was special to them, they had better claim, anything at all, right down to the end tables and the pictures on the walls.

They came, but he thought it was mostly to get a close look at him, to decide for themselves if something was the matter. They had grown up in a house crowded with extra furniture and China figurines, a garage stuffed with the finds from weekend yard sales. They had each spent hours minding the store with its New Guinea masks, Italian Stradivarius knock-off violins, Weimar Theater scholarly books, and antique cash registers. They had each learned how to bargain as buyers and sellers, had come to understand that the family income depended on the gap between what someone would accept to be free of an object and what someone else who craved that same thing would pay. To them, their father's life was a life of stuff.

In fact, it was their mother, Nola, who had inherited a house crammed full of antiques from her great aunt. It was Nola who had said that there would be more money in the estate if they were patient sellers. It was Nola, when she and Christoph were still young, who later reasoned that there might be a living in buying and selling full-time.

Once the children had made sure their father was all right, they looked around, but then didn't take much. The girls had already divided their mother's jewelry. Kent had taken an antique music box. Now Camilla took her mother's silverware, Evelyn claimed a lamp, and Kent rather sheepishly wondered if it would really be all right for him to take two paintings that hung in the living room. "It's now or never," Christoph told him.

"But why now, Dad? Are you sure you're okay?"

"I'm fine," he said. "Better than fine. I've got a buyer for the whole lot of it. The business. All the inventory. I'm selling the house."

Kent said, "That's a big change," as if he were asking a question.

There were contracts to sign, checks to deposit, clothes and dishes and pots and pans to donate. All the acquisitions of a lifetime to dispose of. Then Christoph, with money in the bank, signed the lease on his new apartment, an unfurnished studio close to the library. He'd be able to walk there for books, and walk home to read them. There was a neighborhood market for groceries. Eventually, he'd buy a bed and one set of sheets. He'd buy, probably from one of the thrift shops where he had just donated his things, one spoon, one fork, one knife, one plate, one bowl, one saucepan. He'd buy one chair, or perhaps two, and a table. He'd buy a reading lamp.

Eventually, he'd have to own a few things. A few things were necessary.

But for now, he walked into his little apartment with the clothes on his back, his wallet in one pocket and the apartment key in the other. He lay down on his back on the floor. He took a deep breath, and it seemed to him that it was the deepest breath he had taken in years.

—Bruce Holland Rogers and Stephanie Barbé Hammer

Acknowledgments

This book was made possible by the generous support of 123 backers on Kickstarter. I'm grateful to every one of them for their enthusiasm... and also for their patience when illness, a house fire, and a few other surprises conspired to delay publication.

Four people supported this project as special patrons: Betsy Raymond, Stephanie Barbé Hammer, Carrolle Rushford, and a donor who wished to be identified only as "Muse."

I still owe Betsy Raymond a story that will be written based on three words of her choosing. I either didn't receive her three words in time, or received them and then lost or forgot about them, which would be entirely typical of me. That story will appear in my next collection.

Stephanie Barbé Hammer and I brainstormed the characters of "Everything Must Go" by taking turns writing sentences. The best ideas were hers.

Carrolle Rushford had the right to choose a "product" for me to place in a story; as it turned out, her exercise in "product placement" was anything but commercial. Carrolle asked me to write a story that portrayed spina bifida in a way that would honor her sister. "The Yellow House," grew out of my fictional reimagining and re-purposing of Carrolle's childhood memories.

Muse, a dear friend, fellow writer, and serious patron of the arts, brainstormed with me on what might happen in a story in which Donat Bobet had to deal with the scourge of imaginary termites.

If you read these words in your own limited-edition Kickstarter copy with an embossed first page, Donat Bobet salutes you as a patron of the arts. *Merci pour votre soutien!*

If you have a non-embossed, post-Kickstarter copy of the book, you are no less a patron of the arts. *Merci à vous aussi!* I hope you will join me in appreciating the 123 generous souls who made this book possible.

Finally, thanks to my subscribers at shortshortshort.com. Without you, these stories would not exist.

Made in the USA
Charleston, SC
21 July 2013